Heart

❧

A Summer to Remember

Heartland

Share every moment. . . .

Heartland

A Summer to Remember

by Lauren Brooke

SCHOLASTIC INC.

New York Toronto London Auckland Sydney
Mexico City New Delhi Hong Kong Buenos Aires

ISBN 10: 0-545-04890-7
ISBN 13: 978-0-545-04890-3

Heartland series created by Working Partners Ltd., London.

Copyright © 2008 by Working Partners Ltd.
Published by Scholastic Inc. All rights reserved.

12 11 10 9 8 7 6 5 4 3   8 9 10 11 12 13/0
Printed in the U.S.A.   40
First printing, May 2008

With special thanks to
Elisabeth Faith

Chapter One

"No, Indy, no!" the chestnut pony's rider shouted.

"That's OK. Bring her into the center," Amy Fleming called. She fanned her hand in front of her face as her ten-year-old pupil cantered down the centerline. There was no escaping the intense heat of the midafternoon sun.

Sasha halted Indian Summer in front of Amy. "She just won't strike off on the right leg," she complained. Her auburn curls were damp with perspiration and were sticking to her forehead.

Amy held back a sigh. "I know you want to get Indy to strike off on the correct canter lead wherever you want, but the best place to lead off is in a corner of the arena." Sasha had already made four attempts, ignoring Amy's advice to use the school corners.

1

Sasha narrowed her pale blue eyes. "My parents bought her because her sire was Hideaway's Sebastian, a champion dressage pony. Indy should be able to do something as basic as use the correct canter lead."

Indy can; unfortunately, you *need more practice.* Sasha still wasn't balanced enough in the saddle when she made the transition from trot to canter. Amy placed her hand on the Connemara's neck, which was sticky with sweat. "I don't think we should push her much more today. She's getting hot and tired, and I'm sure you are, too. How about we get her to canter in the corner just so she can finish on a high note? It's really important for her to end each session well so she keeps thinking positively about her schooling."

Sasha hesitated and then nodded. "I guess so."

Amy felt a wave of relief as Sasha trotted the show pony up the centerline, tracked right, and sat deep in the saddle. "Slide your outside leg behind the girth," Amy called. "Keep your inside leg on the girth. Sit deep and keep your hips loose. You should feel her lifting her shoulders and driving forward with her hindquarters."

The pony's ears pricked up as she struck off on the correct leg.

"Well done." Amy congratulated them as Indy cantered perfectly down the long side of the arena.

Indy's breathing came out as a heavy snort with each stride. "OK, I'd like you to walk her on a long rein around the school now so she can cool down and stretch her neck muscles," Amy told Sasha. "She worked hard today."

"That felt really good," her student enthused, leaning forward to pat Indy's shoulder.

Amy smiled. "It was easier for her to strike off on the correct lead from the corner because her weight and balance was on that side."

"I'll keep doing it for a while until she gets the hang of using the correct lead," Sasha said with a nod.

Amy held back a smile at Sasha's determination to think of herself as a star rider and her professionally schooled pony as a novice whenever it came to a move she couldn't do. "That's a great idea," she said instead. "I'm sure it won't be long until she's using the correct lead every time."

Out of the corner of her eye Amy saw Mrs. Madden open the arena gate for her daughter to ride out. "That was terrific," she congratulated Amy as Sasha rode past.

"Thanks," Amy said, watching Sasha ride down to the stable yard. It was clear that the young girl had made steady progress in the first month of her summer lessons with Amy. They watched as Sasha tied Indy to a wall ring outside her stable. Once the mare was secure, she began to untack.

"I know Sash isn't always receptive to instruction. She's always been stubborn, even when she was in diapers!" Mrs. Madden chuckled and pushed her over-size sunglasses farther up the bridge of her nose. "But you really seem to know how to get through to her."

"That's what I'm here for," Amy said with a smile.

Mrs. Madden tucked a stray strand of dyed blond hair behind her ear, looking a little embarrassed all of a sudden. She looked over at Sasha and then back at Amy with an imploring look on her face. "Sasha thinks you're so wonderful. She took a poster off her bedroom wall before coming for her lesson and she'd love you to autograph it. Sash has told all her friends that she's having lessons with Heartland's Amy Fleming!"

Amy felt herself turn red. It was surprising how many people discovered her association with Heartland even when she was away from home. She felt a tug of remorse for staying near Virginia Tech for the summer instead of going back to Heartland. But she wanted to earn the extra credit by teaching on the riding yard attached to the university. It would be so useful when she was back at Heartland if she were a qualified riding instructor. *I just wish I could still see Grandpa, Lou, and Holly.* The last time Amy had seen her niece was at her first birthday party over spring break.

Amy walked down to the Maddens' dark blue Jeep. Mrs. Madden opened the back door and took the poster off the backseat. She unrolled it to reveal a blown-up photograph of Indy cantering across a paddock. The mare's chestnut tail streamed behind her like a banner and her mane whipped away from her proudly arched neck.

"It's beautiful," Amy said admiringly.

"Would you believe I stood in the field taking different shots for about an hour before I got this one? We had the local photo shop blow it up for us," Mrs. Madden commented with a wry smile. She held out a pen, and Amy carefully signed her name in the bottom corner.

"Oh, you signed it. Great!" Sasha cried, beaming as she joined them. "I put Indy into her stall with her rugs on," she told Amy.

"Perfect," Amy said. "I'll see you same time next week. Keep practicing that canter."

"In the corners." Sasha nodded. She wiped her arm over her forehead. "It's so hot! Mom, did you bring a soda?"

"In the glove compartment," Mrs. Madden told her. "See you next week, Amy, and thanks again."

"Yeah, thanks," Sasha called over her shoulder as she climbed into the Jeep.

Amy waved good-bye as they drove off. *A cold drink with extra ice would hit the spot right now!* She walked across the yard and paused at Indy's stall. The mare was resting her hind leg as she pulled at her hay net. "Good work today," Amy told her. Indy swung her head around at the sound of Amy's voice and gave a low whicker.

Amy checked that the mare's water was full and then left her to her feed. The stalls were all occupied because the horses were kept in during the heat of the day and let out at night. As she walked the length of the livery stable block, some of the horses looked over their doors at the sound of her footsteps. "Hey, George, Shamrock, Lily," Amy greeted them. For once she resisted the temptation to stop and stroke their noses. Getting something to drink and hopping in the shower were her priorities at this point.

She turned the corner of the stable block and followed the path that led to the building where she was staying for the summer. The riding school staff all got to stay in a set of beautiful old brick buildings. They were the original stables on the yard but had been converted when the new stable block was built.

Amy pushed open the yellow-painted door of the second cottage in the row. Now that she'd been staying here for ten weeks, she definitely felt at home. She kicked off her boots and padded over the cool oak-boarded floor. The downstairs had a long, low-roofed living room that opened into a small kitchen. Amy went right to the fridge and pulled out a soda. She snapped back the top and gulped down the ice-cold drink with a sigh of relief.

There were no signs of her roommates, Tamsin and Ellen. Tamsin was a full-time instructor at the yard, and Ellen was one of the stable hands. Amy realized

Tamsin was probably visiting her boyfriend since it was her afternoon off, while Ellen was most likely preparing the evening feeds. *Once I shower and check my e-mail, I'll go see if she needs a hand.*

After her shower, Amy sat down in the small study area that was tucked off to one side near the staircase. While she was waiting for her laptop to boot up, she looked up at the bulletin board and smiled at the latest picture of Holly she'd tacked up as decoration. Her niece was sitting in her high chair waving two chocolate-coated hands at the camera. Other photos of Holly, Lou and Scott's wedding day, Grandpa Jack, and Amy's best friend, Soraya, left hardly any space for the summer reading list that also hung on the board. She glanced at one of the textbooks that she had left open on the desk. Not too many people stuck around school over the summer, so Amy had had most of her nights to herself. She usually spent the time getting ahead in her reading. It was a quiet way to spend the summer, but Amy enjoyed her studies so much she didn't really mind.

Amy signed in to her e-mail account and smiled when she saw new mail from her college friend Will Savage. She was touched that he'd kept in touch all summer even though he was on vacation in Europe with his girlfriend, Sharona Michaels. She leaned forward to read his message.

Amy felt a twinge of regret that she wasn't off seeing

new things like her college friends were. She thought back to the time more than a year ago when she had joined Will at a cattle ranch in Arizona. Apart from working with the ranch vet to earn credits for their course, Will had asked her to help out with one of the horses there who had lost his trust in people. It was at the end of that trip that Amy had made the decision to break up with her longtime boyfriend, Ty. That was when she'd had to admit that their lives were moving in separate directions.

Just as she was finishing Will's e-mail, a new message flashed up on the screen. Amy frowned as she read the sender's name. *Alfredo Escobar?* She was about to send the mail to her junk folder but then realized that the name wasn't totally unfamiliar. *I think I met him at Mi-Ya's party last term.* Her college friend had thrown an end-of-term bash in her room and had invited some of her friends from outside Virginia Tech. Amy had spent time chatting with Alfredo after Mi-Ya had mentioned that he played polo on a professional team and owned a string of polo horses. He was Argentinean, if she remembered correctly, and his dark features and olive skin had made an impression on Amy. She recalled how nice it had been to hear the slight accent that came from learning English as his second language.

Feeling more than a bit curious, she opened up his mail.

Hi, Amy,

I hope you don't mind, I got your e-mail address from Mi-Ya. We met at her party before the vacation.

I know this is out of the blue, but I'd really like your advice. Do you remember me telling you about the youngest mare on my team — Impala? She's the five-year-old that I've been training for the last two years. This summer I started to ride her in matches, but she's not taking to the game the way she should. She's fine to ride and train in the arena, but the moment she's in with other horses and is expected to take part in the whole stick-and-ball routine, she flips. I've tried everything. I've had a veterinarian and a horse dentist check her over to see if she's in any pain but they couldn't find anything. All of her tack has been replaced and the new tack has been carefully fitted. Physically, there's nothing wrong with her, but she's still playing-up on the field.

Yesterday my coach told me to drop Impala from my team ☹. That's why I'm mailing you. I really don't want to give up on her — when she's not on the polo field, she shows amazing potential — but I'm at a loss for what to do next. Is there any way you'd be able to take a look at her? If you can make the trip to our stables in the Hamptons, I'll pay all your expenses — you'll be doing me a huge favor. The way you spoke about your work made me think that you might be able to make a breakthrough with Impala. Is there a chance you can help?

My fingers are crossed,
Alfredo Escobar

Amy glanced at the address and telephone number at the bottom of the note and then sat back in her chair. The Hamptons! It was an incredibly tempting offer, but she was supposed to spend this summer earning her instruction credit. Maybe she could complete her remaining hours sooner than she'd planned and then she could fly out and work with Impala.

Her heart raced with excitement at the thought of traveling to Alfredo's place and working with his horses. It seemed likely that Impala's issues were linked to some aspect of the sport, since she misbehaved only when she was playing. *Maybe I should find out a little about polo before I give this too much thought.*

She sat forward again and entered the word *polo* into a search engine. When the results popped up she clicked on one Web site and was shocked to see the pages and pages of information included. This was a complicated sport! But when she looked at the photos of the specially bred horses galloping across a pitch, their riders holding mallets high in the air, she felt a fresh rush of excitement.

Amy jumped up. She definitely had to try to negotiate leaving the yard before the end of her agreed time. Since she had already passed all of her supervised and observed teaching sessions, all that remained was completing the hours needed to get her credit. She decided to go see the yard owner, Sal Harrow, to discuss how many more hours she needed to put in.

Amy pulled on her boots and hurried over to Sal's office. Her feet crunched over the gravel that had been put down for easy maintenance. As she walked past the office windows she could see Sal inside working at her desk.

Sal looked up and waved when she noticed Amy outside. "Come right in, the door's open," she called.

Amy made her way into the office building and went right through to the shelf-lined study that Sal used as her office.

"Hey, Amy," Sal said as Amy entered the room. "How are things?"

"Good, thanks," Amy said. "You have such a terrific view," she said admiringly as she looked out the window. "I bet it takes some of the sting out of having to do paperwork!"

Acres of grazing land stretched into the distance. The azure sky rose against the tree-lined horizon without a single cloud to spoil the sweep of blue. Over to the left were the cottages for the staff and beyond that was the stable yard.

"It's true, especially when the horses are turned out," Sal agreed. She pushed a hand through her short dark hair and placed the pen she'd been using down on the desk. "So," she said, gesturing for Amy to take a seat in the chair facing her, "what's up? Trouble with a student?"

"No," Amy said quickly. "I finished with Sasha an hour ago and she was thrilled that she finally cantered on the correct leg."

"Great," Sal said warmly. "You're a natural teacher, Amy. If you find out that being a vet isn't for you, I'd hire you in a heartbeat. In fact, I just finished writing up your final observed teaching session and said pretty much the same thing in my comments."

"Thanks, Sal," Amy said, and smiled. She thought for a moment of her long-term dream to combine veterinary skills with alternative healing. "But I don't think I'll ever have second thoughts about being a vet." She took a deep breath before starting to explain why she'd come by the office. "There's actually something else I need to talk with you about. I got an e-mail today from a friend of a friend. He lives out in the Hamptons. You might have heard of his family — the Escobars?"

Sal's eyebrows shot up. "Are you kidding? They're one of the most famous teams on the polo circuit! They breed amazing horses, all descendants of their first stallion."

Amy's pulse quickened. "Well, Alfredo Escobar wrote to ask if I could fly up and take a look at one of his horses.

She's misbehaving on the pitch and he can't figure out why." She paused before posing her big question. "Is there any way we can arrange for me to complete my instruction credit early?"

Sal looked at Amy for a moment and then looked down at the desk before her. Amy watched as the yard owner chewed on her lower lip, clearly mulling over the request. "I'm not happy at the thought of losing you," Sal said ruefully. "But this opportunity is too good to pass by. Not only will you be getting up close and personal with some legendary horses, but a chance to spend part of your summer in the Hamptons doesn't come along every day. My only concern is if you'll ever be able to come back to the reality of Virginia after being there." With that, Sal's face broke into a huge smile.

Amy grinned back. "I'll try to keep my feet on the ground," she promised.

Sal's face became serious again, and she drummed her fingertips against the arms of her chair. "If I give you a few extra classes out of this week's schedule, then I'm pretty sure that by Thursday you'll have completed the hours you need to get your instruction credit," she said.

That would give Amy three days of heavy teaching. If she arranged with Alfredo to fly to the Hamptons that weekend, she wouldn't have much time to get ready. But she would make it work if it meant that she would be able to go. Flying out at the end of the week would give her almost a whole month to work with Impala before she'd have to come back to get ready for school. "Thanks, Sal," she said. "I really appreciate that. I won't let you down."

"You've worked hard for the past month and you should get to have some fun. You totally deserve to finish off your vacation in a whirl of Thoroughbreds and high society," Sal joked.

Amy laughed. "That sounds like the title of a bad movie."

Sal stood up. "I think I've done enough paperwork for now. Do you want to join me for a break?"

"Sure," Amy agreed. She followed Sal out into a large kitchen that was being kept cool by two quietly turning ceiling fans.

Sal opened one of the white-painted cupboard doors, reached in, and brought out two glasses. She set them down on the shiny black counter before heading over to the fridge. "What can I get you?"

"An iced tea would be great if there is some. Thanks." Amy sat up on one of the leather-topped chrome bar stools.

As soon as she had poured them both drinks, Sal joined Amy at the counter. "So, I hope you're packing an autograph book."

Amy blinked. "Are the Escobars really that famous?"

"No," Sal laughed. "I'm talking about all the real celebrities who head out to their homes in the Hamptons every summer. Anyone who lives near the Escobars will be seriously wealthy." She reached over to give Amy a hug. "Just promise that you'll take a break from having the time of your life long enough to send me some pictures!"

Chapter Two

❧

Amy was at her gate in the airport and was just about to turn her cell phone off when it began to ring. She grinned when she saw Lou's name on the display screen.

"Hi, sis."

"Hey. I wasn't sure what time your flight was, but Holly wanted to talk to her favorite aunt one more time." Lou's voice was bright.

"Her *only* aunt." Amy smiled. "You're lucky, I was just about to board."

"*You're* the lucky one. You don't have to wipe doughy handprints off the phone when you hang up. We're in the middle of baking Daddy some cookies, aren't we, sweetheart? Say hi to Auntie Amy."

There was a fumbling on the other end of the line and then Holly's sweet voice said, "Ba-ba."

"Hello, Holly. How are you? Auntie Amy can't wait to see you," Amy promised, feeling a surge of longing to see her little niece again.

Lou came back on. "Send me some pictures as soon as you can. I'm so jealous that you're getting to hang out with the rich and famous while I stay here and bake cookies."

"Liar, you love it." Amy knew how much her sister adored spending time with Holly. "I've got to go, they're boarding the plane. Give Holly, Scott, and Grandpa kisses from me, OK?"

"Sure. Have a great time," Lou said. "I'll talk to you soon."

Amy turned off her phone. Staying at the Hamptons was going to have to be everything she was hoping and more to ease the homesickness she was feeling right now. She shouldered her carry-on and got in line to board the plane. This was no good. She had to focus on why she was going to the Escobars'. *I just hope that I can help Impala. Alfredo's counting on me.*

☬

Alfredo had arranged for Amy to be picked up just past the baggage claim at Islip airport. Amy walked down a line of drivers, scanning the cards they held with names printed on them until she saw hers being held by a chauffeur dressed in a gray uniform and matching cap.

"Miss Fleming?" the chauffeur asked as she walked up to him.

Amy nodded.

"I'd like to welcome you to New York on behalf of the Escobars. May I take your luggage?" The chauffeur held out his hand for Amy's suitcase and led her to a black limousine. He opened the rear door and Amy tried to hold back her wide grin as she slid onto the polished leather interior. The moment the door closed she leaned her head back and breathed in the smell of the upholstery.

The car pulled away so smoothly that Amy only realized they were moving when the scenery began to change. She closed her eyes, suddenly feeling tired after the whirlwind of activity over the last few days. She'd taken over Sal's basic dressage classes and a jumping class along with three more private sessions. It had been hectic and she'd hardly had time to write her reports on her teaching, but she'd managed to complete all the hours she needed for her instruction credit.

When she opened her eyes again she was surprised at just how rural the scenery was. They were driving past beautiful homes and sprawling green lawns. A few fields were full of sleek, long-legged Thoroughbred horses, sheltering from the sun under large, spreading trees. They turned onto a coastal road for a few miles and Amy caught a glimpse of a flotilla of sailboats on the horizon just as the road turned and headed back inland.

The limousine slowed in front of a magnificent pair of wrought-iron gates. Amy noticed two cameras mounted on a post. It looked like security was pretty tight on this estate. A shiver of excitement raced through her at the thought of meeting the horses.

The gates slowly swung back, and the limousine drove up a long driveway. Amy hit the button to roll the window down and her hair whipped back as she leaned out. White-painted fences lined each side of the drive, enclosing acres of lush pastureland. Huge elm and beech trees cast blue-green pools of shade, although the fields were empty. Amy was disappointed not to see any horses right away. *They must be in the stable, away from the heat,* she thought.

The road forked and the limousine turned right. They left the paved road and crunched onto a gravel driveway. The car rounded another bend and the main house came into view. Amy caught her breath. In their e-mails to arrange her visit, Alfredo hadn't prepared her for the fact that he lived in a mansion! The colonial-style house had balconies running the entire length of the second floor and the trellises between each one were completely covered with climbing red roses. The white house gleamed in the sun, and Amy had to blink against the bright reflection.

The car came to a stop by a flight of steps leading to a huge set of open double doors. Amy admired the two marble horses' heads set on pillars on either side of the entrance. Just then, a lady with graying hair walked out of the house. Amy started to let herself out of the car and stopped just as the chauffeur came around to open the door for her.

"Thanks," she said.

"I hope you enjoy your stay," he replied. "Please, go ahead inside and I'll make sure your luggage makes it to your room."

Amy thanked him again and then headed up the stone steps.

"Hello, Miss Fleming. Did you have a good flight?" the lady at the top of the steps said as Amy approached.

"Yes, thanks," Amy said, wondering who the woman was. "Please, call me Amy." She took in the woman's black dress and neat pearl earrings and guessed she was probably Alfredo's grandmother.

"I'm Ellen, the housekeeper," the lady said before Amy had a chance to say anything else. She held out a silver tray with a glass of ice water. "May I offer you a drink?"

"That's great, thanks," Amy said as she sipped the cool water, aware that her vocabulary currently seemed limited to "thanks." "This is an amazing house."

"Mrs. Escobar has completely transformed it over the last few years," Ellen told her as she led the way inside. Her heels clacked over the mosaic-tiled floor of the cavernous entrance hall. A staircase curved up the wall and natural light flooded in from a window at the top.

Ellen put the tray on a polished oval table in the center of the hall. "I'll take you up to your room so you can freshen up. Carlos will bring your bags."

Amy followed Ellen up the staircase. She would have loved to stop and study the gilt-framed oil paintings hanging along the wall, but thought it would be rude not to keep up with Ellen.

At the top of the stairs, Ellen turned down a burgundy-carpeted hallway. They passed a half-dozen doors, and Amy wondered just how many bedrooms the mansion held. Ellen paused outside a cream-painted door facing them at the end of the corridor. "This is your room."

Amy tried not to gape too obviously as she stepped into the room. The voile curtains of the four-poster bed shifted gently against the breeze from the open veranda windows. There were two floor-to-ceiling wardrobes for Amy to hang her clothes in, and a dressing table with a large, lighted mirror. A deep-wine-colored armchair in the far corner of the room complemented the luxurious cream of the walls and carpet.

Ellen opened a door opposite the bed and gestured to the large bathroom beyond it. "Would you like me to run you a bath?"

"Um, I'm good, thanks," Amy told her. "I thought I might go down to the yard and find Alfredo."

"Oh, he won't be there now," Ellen said. "He rides before the heat of the day. He's more likely to be swimming. I'll let him know that you've arrived. If you need anything, just let me know."

Amy got the feeling it would be perfectly normal around here for her to lie back on the bed and ring a silver bell to order a cup of tea. *Somehow, I don't see that happening!* She laughed to herself. The Escobars might be waited on hand and foot, but Amy couldn't remember a time when she hadn't wanted to take care of her own needs. She waited as Ellen left the room before she wandered out onto the room's veranda. The air was heavy with the scent from the climbing roses on the trellis. Amy inhaled deeply as she leaned over the balcony's edge and looked out over the Escobar estate. The driveway circled the yard like a giant horseshoe. From her balcony, she could see the red-tiled roofs of three large barns. Around the back of the nearest barn, and facing her, was a row of stables with an overhanging roof. She counted six stalls, three of which had horses looking out over their doors.

She had a feeling that the Escobar horses had a completely luxurious, pampered life. *And yet Alfredo's description of Impala's behavior doesn't fit with the idea that she's a happy horse,* Amy considered. The sooner she got to meet the mare, the sooner she could begin figuring out what was making her act up.

She glanced down at the button-down shirt and capri pants she was wearing and figured she'd be fine keeping them on to go say hi to Impala. She didn't feel comfortable putting on her old yard clothes in such opulent surroundings! She'd find Alfredo and ask him to take her out to the barns.

She padded over the soft carpet and retraced her way to the entrance hall. Five doors opened off the circular hallway and she hesitated, unsure of which one to choose. She jumped as the grandfather clock chimed three times. Looking at the enormous clock, Amy noticed a huge glass cabinet. Each shelf inside was full of silver cups and plates. Amy walked over and read some of the inscriptions on the trophies. They were all commemorating first- and second-place performances by Team Escobar.

Amy glanced at the nearest set of double doors. Since Alfredo still hadn't made an appearance, she figured she might as well go and wait for him in the closest room.

As she entered the room, her first thought was that it deserved a spread in *Better Homes and Gardens* magazine. Heavy brocade drapes were tied back from French doors that opened onto the yard and allowed sunlight to pool on the polished wooden floorboards. Three gold-and-wine-striped sofas were placed around a fireplace at the far end of the room, and gorgeous armchairs were strategically placed with lamps for reading. Amy sat down on the sofa facing the fireplace and picked up a polo magazine from an oak coffee table.

"You won't find anything of interest to you in there," a thickly accented voice said. "Just straightforward, honest technique."

Amy was so startled, she almost dropped the magazine. She'd thought she was alone.

A deeply lined face looked at her from one of the high-backed chairs along the wall. "You're the girl Alfredo asked here, no? You've come to do your mind tricks on Impala." The man slowly stood up. Amy was struck by the brightness of his dark eyes under a set of bushy gray eyebrows. He folded the newspaper he'd been reading and tossed it down on his chair. He picked up his walking stick and leaned heavily on it, looking menacingly at Amy. "It's not our way. It's never been our way."

Amy's cheeks burned. "That's not the way I work, either," she started to explain.

"Then you think you can train Impala better than Alfredo? Is that it? What do you know about polo, exactly?" The old man's intense gaze never moved off Amy's face.

"Amy!" She turned just in time to see Alfredo hurry into the room.

Amy felt butterflies in her stomach and was momentarily speechless. She had forgotten just how good-looking Alfredo was.

"I'm so sorry I missed your arrival. I lost track of time." His black hair was wet and had been combed back. "We were out at the pool." Alfredo's voice was smooth and his accent gave it an exotic sound. Amy noticed that his navy breeches were cut perfectly to fit his muscular legs, and his dark green polo shirt draped perfectly over his broad shoulders. TEAM ESCO-BAR was embroidered underneath a beautiful horse's head on the top left of the shirt. Amy suddenly wished that she'd changed into her riding clothes. Her cheeks grew hot when she realized she'd been staring at Alfredo for several seconds without saying anything.

"You waste too much time, always!" said the older man, who was still leaning on his cane at the edge of the room. He raised his eyes to the ceiling. "When I was your age I didn't do all this, what do you call it? *Chilling.* I trained all day, and when I wasn't training, I was thinking about training!"

Alfredo smiled at Amy and gestured to the grouchy man. "Amy, this is my grandfather," he said. "Papa, you remember — Amy has come to help sort Impala out?"

"Sort her out?" Papa grumbled. "There's nothing wrong with that mare that an experienced hand couldn't fix. None of the other horses bred and trained on this yard have ever had such problems." He headed back to his chair and made a fuss of shaking out his newspaper before sitting back down to read.

Alfredo's dark brows furrowed. He shot Amy an apologetic look as he led her back to the sofa. "Papa doesn't play polo anymore, but he still takes a lot of interest in the team. It was Papa who began the family team when he bought his first stallion. . . ."

"Manticore," Amy murmured.

Alfredo smiled. "You've done your research."

"Sal, the owner of the riding school I worked at this summer, told me," Amy confessed.

"That's him." Alfredo nodded at a painting over the fireplace. A Thoroughbred chestnut stallion stood in profile with his head turned to look proudly out of the picture. He had a sloping shoulder, a short back, and muscular quarters. His head was refined and intelligent-looking with large, bold eyes. Amy glanced again at the horse's head on Alfredo's polo shirt. It was the same horse.

"It's such an unusual name," she said. "Is it Argentinean?"

"It comes from Persian legend, actually. The manticore was a beast with the body of a red lion and a human head with three rows of sharp teeth. Its name means man-eater, which gives you an idea of the Escobar sense of humor." Alfredo grinned, his teeth white against his tanned skin. "Papa bred Manticore with South American Criollo mares, which are famous for their endurance," he went on. "His descendants have been sold all over the world, for sport as well as for work."

Amy nodded. "You can see that he'd sire amazing foals."

"How?" demanded a gruff voice from the shadows.

Amy started. She'd almost forgotten that Papa was in the room.

"What do you know about the breeding that goes into polo ponies?" The old man's dark brown eyes bored into her as he leaned forward. Amy knew she was being challenged and she took a deep breath.

"His head, neck, and shoulders look strong. He has a well-sprung rib cage and plenty of heart and lung room. His hindquarters are sturdy and his legs are clean. Everything about him suggests symmetry and balance. I know I don't have any experience with polo, but I do know what makes a good horse."

Papa's eyes narrowed. "All of the Escobar horses are good. But how will you know that if Alfredo keeps you cooped up inside? Alfredo, take your guest to the stables."

Amy felt some of her tension ease at the thought of heading outside.

"Sure thing, Papa," Alfredo agreed. He winked at Amy, and led the way out of the room.

"Did you want to get changed into your yard clothes?" Alfredo asked.

Amy looked down at her shirt and cropped trousers. "I didn't feel right putting on my old jeans and T-shirt," she confessed.

Alfredo nodded. "I always feel like I'm going to smudge the furniture, even when my clothes are clean." His brown eyes twinkled. "My stepmom runs an interior design business and she's refurbished most of the rooms in the house. I haven't let her get her hands on my rooms, though! Let's just say I prefer the lived-in look."

"It's all the rage in college." Amy laughed, thinking of the room she shared with India last year. It had often looked more like a changing room than a bedroom, what with clothes scattered everywhere. She could feel herself beginning to relax. "I'll need a couple of minutes to get changed."

"I'm going to get a glass of water. Meet me in the kitchen," Alfredo told her, pointing to the double doors beyond the staircase.

Amy hurried upstairs and found her suitcase just inside the door. She picked out her yard clothes and quickly got changed. Carrying her boots, she headed back downstairs and went in search of Alfredo.

The kitchen was tiled in warm terra-cotta hues, and dried herbs hung from a beam that ran the width of the ceiling. Amy detected the heady scent of lavender. It was a smell she associated with Heartland

and the many times she'd used it to calm stressed animals.

Alfredo was washing a glass at the sink. "Ready?"

She nodded. "This is a great kitchen." She loved the worn oak fittings and the white stone sink.

"My stepmom calls it the distressed rural look. You'd be surprised by how much her clients pay to get a worn-out-looking kitchen," Alfredo joked. The back door out of the kitchen was just like a stable door. The top half was already hooked open and Alfredo now opened the bottom section.

Amy followed him onto a patio lined with large troughs filled with herbs. A tall, slender woman with long, dark hair held back by a red bandanna was watering one of the boxes.

"Hey, Susannah," Alfredo said. "Amy's here." He turned to Amy. "I'd like you to meet my stepmom."

"Thanks so much for having me in your beautiful home," Amy said, stepping forward. She hoped that Alfredo's stepmother was happier about her visit than his grandfather had been.

Susannah put down the watering can and gave Amy a warm smile. "It's a pleasure, Amy. Alfredo was so pleased when you agreed to come. You must treat the place as your own home while you're here." Her voice was gentle and only slightly tinged with a South American accent.

"Thank you," Amy said, relaxing. Susannah seemed genuinely pleased to see her.

"You must use the pool as often as you want, and the home-movie theater is always cool if the heat gets to be too much."

"From what I've heard about Amy, I'm going to have a hard time getting her away from the yard," Alfredo said jokingly.

"Hey, I'm not a workaholic. I can *chill* with the best of them," Amy teased.

"Good, Amy. I learned long ago not to let the men of this house crack the whip," Susannah joined in.

Amy smiled. While she loved the idea of having easy access to a pool and movie theater, Alfredo was closer to the truth than he knew. Right now she couldn't think of anywhere she wanted to be more than the Escobar stable yard!

Chapter Three

❧

As Amy approached the yard, she realized that it was much bigger than she had thought when she first saw it from her balcony. Alfredo led her past a grazing area and pointed down a paved path. "Down there are indoor and outdoor arenas and the horse pool. The staff housing and parking lot are behind the broodmare barn on the main yard."

"You have a horse pool?" Amy questioned. Although she'd studied the benefits of swimming on animal joints, she'd never actually seen a real pool for horses.

"Yes. We use it to improve fitness and performance and to help the horses recover from injuries. I'll show you sometime, if you'd like."

"I'd like that very much." Amy smiled.

With a sudden clatter of hooves, a chestnut stallion trotted out from under a redbrick arch onto the path just ahead.

"Dad!" Alfredo called to the rider.

The man on the horse glanced over his shoulder and then reined the stallion around. Amy caught her breath as the horse approached. His neck was arched and he carried his tail high. His coat gleamed like polished mahogany and his dark eyes shone with intelligence.

"He's just like Manticore," Amy commented, looking at the stallion's powerful quarters and sloping shoulder.

"He *is* Manticore," Alfredo replied. "Or at least, his great-great-great-grandson."

Alfredo's father halted the stallion. "It's an Escobar tradition," he explained. "Ever since the first Manticore, we've always named one of his descendants on the yard Manticore. It brings us luck." He transferred his reins and polo mallet to one hand and held out the other. "You must be Amy. I'm Pablo." The resemblance between Pablo and Papa was immediately visible in his bushy eyebrows and bright eyes. Pablo also had an Argentinean accent that lent a lyrical quality to his speech.

Amy shook his gloved hand. "It's good to meet you."

"You, too," Pablo replied. "Alfredo's told us all about your work. I'd love to watch you at some point — if you wouldn't mind."

"It would be fine," Amy said, delighted that Alfredo's father was interested in her methods instead of sharing Papa's skepticism.

Manticore snorted and tossed his head. "He wants to run off some energy." Pablo patted Manticore's shoulder. "Just one minute, boy." His eyes turned serious. "The vet's been out to see Elvira. It's as we thought, she's strained the tendon."

"Oh, no," Alfredo said, and groaned. "She's off your string, then."

Pablo nodded. "Once she's recovered, she can join the broodmares. I have to decide whether to put in some intensive training on Aspire or buy a replacement."

"Aspire's still green," Alfredo mused. "Do you think she can cope with the pressure of the circuit so soon?"

"I wouldn't have to use her as long as the rest of the string remained injury free," Pablo said. "But I'm not sure she's up to the rigors of a match if I did have to use her. I'm leaning toward buying an experienced player."

Alfredo turned to Amy. "Dad has seven horses on his team. Elvira was one of his best players but she popped her leg yesterday. Once a horse strains a tendon, it can't ever do anything as rigorous as playing polo again. We need to replace her, but none of our new ponies are ready to join this summer's circuit. Aspire's one of our youngsters in training." He sighed and turned back to Pablo.

"I think it would be safer to buy something with a couple of years' experience."

Pablo nodded. "We'll talk about it some more later." He returned his attention to Amy. "I look forward to seeing you at dinner." He reined Manticore back around and swung his mallet up in the air as he trotted toward the arenas.

"It's such bad timing," Alfredo said as he turned onto a wide gravel track. "Dad's going to hate retiring Elvira. The last thing we need is to have problems with *another* member of the team."

They walked under a huge redbrick arch supported by two pillars. Amy took in a breath as they walked onto the yard. The three horse barns were connected by redbrick archways and the middle barn had a huge clock face set above its double doors. *This is some setup!* she marveled to herself.

"Hey, Alfredo," a stable hand called as he walked by, pushing a bale of hay in a wheelbarrow.

"Hey, Joe." Alfredo nodded to the dark-haired man. "This is Amy Fleming. She's come to help me out with Impala."

"Hey, Amy." Joe put down the barrow and held out his hand. "Nice to meet you."

Amy smiled. "You, too."

"Chrissie's in with Archie," Joe said to Alfredo. "The

farrier arrived about ten minutes ago to work on his front shoe."

"One of my horses threw a shoe this morning," Alfredo explained to Amy.

"Wow, that was a quick response from the farrier," Amy said.

"He comes out to us twice a week," Alfredo replied. "We've got more than sixty horses on the yard, so there's always something for him to deal with." He nodded to the barn on their right. "That's the broodmares' barn, and up there," he indicated straight ahead, "is where we keep the yearlings."

As he spoke, a stable hand walked out of the yearlings' barn, leading a long-legged filly. "In the summer we keep the horses in for the hottest part of the day," Alfredo went on. "They're about to be turned back out now."

"Do you want a hand leading your string out?" Amy said.

Alfredo looked surprised, but then smiled as if Amy had made a joke. "Chrissie sees to my turnout."

Another yearling clattered out onto the yard and Amy was happy for the distraction. *Of course he doesn't do his own turnout*, she thought. *There are more than enough people working here to cover that.* This wasn't Heartland, where all hands were needed to keep the yard going.

"Our polo ponies are kept over here," Alfredo continued.

They headed toward the barn. The door was open, and the bay and palomino in the nearest stalls pricked up their ears as Amy and Alfredo approached.

"My uncle and cousin keep their horses here along with my father's and mine," Alfredo said as they walked into the barn. Toward the end of the aisle, a stable hand was holding a bay gelding while a farrier bent over his front hoof.

Alfredo stopped outside the palomino's stall. "This is Nial, one of my father's horses."

"Hey, Nial." Amy held her hand in front of the bars for the palomino to sniff. "You're a gorgeous boy, aren't you?"

The gelding snorted.

"And he knows it!" Alfredo laughed. He nodded at the horses on the opposite side of the aisle. "That's my cousin Jaime's string."

Just then the farrier began to tap the bay gelding's hoof. The bay threw his head up in the air and tried to pull away.

"Stand, Archie, there's a good boy," the stable girl said soothingly. She shortened the lead rope.

"Archie had a leg injury a few months ago. He's still wary about having anyone go near it even though he's totally recovered," Alfredo told Amy.

They walked down a few stalls and stopped. A pretty bay mare was lying down on a thick bed of hay.

"Elvira?" Amy guessed, looking at the bandage on the mare's front leg.

The mare raised her head at the sound of Amy's voice. She shifted her hind legs in the straw as if she were about to get up.

"Come on." Alfredo tugged at Amy's sleeve. "She'll try to come over to see if we have a treat if we stay here."

From the opposite aisle, one of the other horses kicked the door, eager for his share of attention.

"Does your uncle live here, too?" Amy asked. She crossed over to scratch the forehead of the black gelding who, like the rest of the Escobar horses, had a muscular body with a strongly developed neck.

"No. Papa always assumed that my uncle Juan, as the eldest, would take over for him. But it was my dad who showed the most interest in the running of the estate. Both Juan and Jaime live and work in New York City, but they come here most weekends and never miss any of our matches."

"So who rides their horses when they're not here?" Amy stroked the black gelding's velvety nose.

"All of the stable hands are experienced riders," Alfredo replied. "They work under Ricardo's instruction." He walked back across the aisle. "He's our coach."

They headed slowly along the stable aisle. Alfredo

introduced each of the horses as they went and finally came to a stop at the last stall in the row.

Amy joined him at the door. A pony was dozing in the middle of the stall. She had a bright chestnut coat and a white star on her forehead, its edges sharp and clear against the flame-colored hair. The mare opened her eyes and gazed at them.

"This is Impala. Dad gave her to me before she was born," Alfredo said. "There's no other polo pony in the world who can beat her bloodline. It's why I can't blame her for not performing properly. It has to be something I've done, right?" A muscle jumped in his cheek.

Amy put her hand on his arm. "I wouldn't be so quick to blame her training. There's no point until we have a look at what exactly she's doing wrong."

Alfredo's eyes widened at Amy's touch. She dropped her hand away, cheeks burning. For some reason she felt as if she knew Alfredo better than she actually did, and touching him had seemed totally natural. But as she realized what she'd done, she felt embarrassed.

"She followed the same training schedule as all of the other horses," Alfredo agreed, turning to Impala. He clicked to Impala, who looked steadily at him. "Clever girl." Alfredo smiled. "She thinks she's going to get ridden, so she's not moving. She's telling us it's too hot to go out!"

Amy looked at the mare. Nothing about her appeared uptight or stressed. She was resting her hind leg and her body was relaxed. *Whatever is making her unhappy doesn't seem present in her home environment,* Amy thought.

"Come on, Impala," Alfredo urged. He slid back the door and held out his hand.

The mare rustled through her straw bed and stretched out her neck to sniff at Alfredo's hand. She snorted in disappointment when she found it was empty.

"Hey, girl." Amy bent her head to blow in Impala's nostrils. The mare blew back. Amy reached up to stroke Impala's velvety nose. "It's their way of saying hello," she explained to Alfredo.

The moment Amy stopped fussing, the mare scraped at the ground with her hoof. Amy chuckled. "You like that?" She scratched Impala's temple, and the mare closed her eyes. "She's lovely," she said to Alfredo.

He patted Impala's neck. "Her disposition's great," he agreed. "It's one of the reasons why her behavior doesn't make any sense. I've considered every possible cause. She's been checked over by a vet, an osteopath, a dentist. She's been in the pool; she's been given a rest. I've replaced every piece of her tack. Nothing has made a difference. The moment she's on that polo field, she acts up." Amy noticed Alfredo's fingers were digging into his palm.

"Could she be scared of the game?" she asked. "I'd imagine it could be pretty scary with the noise and action."

Alfredo shook his head. "Ricardo thought that, so he turned her loose in the arena while Dad, Juan, Jaime, and I played. You should have seen her, Amy. She chased us around, her tail kinked, and her eyes were shining. She was sired by Manticore out of Blossom. She was *born* to play. It's in her blood. Anyway, it's a bad trainer who blames his horse. I keep coming back to it being something about her training that I did wrong." He bit his lip, and Amy could feel his tension. "How about we get her tacked up? You can check her out in the arena."

Amy ran her hand down the mare's satiny neck. *Alfredo sounds like he's expecting me to find a quick fix,* she thought. "Getting to know Impala is a huge part of helping her work through her problem. I'd like to spend some time with her before I ride in the arena, if that's OK." More than anything, she didn't want rushing into things to prevent her from figuring out what was going on.

Alfredo blinked in surprise. "How about a trail ride, then?" he said after a moment of consideration.

"Sounds perfect," Amy said.

Chapter Four

❧

Amy lifted Impala's English-style saddle off its rack.
The leather was supple and smelled freshly cleaned. She
hooked the mare's bridle over her shoulder and then
turned to Alfredo, who was pulling together Archie's
tack. "Should I go ahead?" Amy asked.

"Sure," Alfredo said.

Impala's stall was alongside the tack room. Amy slid
the door open. "Back. There's a good girl." She clicked
to Impala, who was blocking her way in. Impala took two
steps back, enough for Amy to enter the stall and slide the
door closed. Even though Impala's chestnut coat gleamed,
Amy had picked up a sheepskin mitt to run over her.

"Stand still, beautiful," she encouraged.

Impala stretched to sniff the mitt. "It will feel good,"
Amy promised. "You just relax, OK?"

Impala stood quietly while Amy drew the mitt down her neck and over her shoulder. As she worked, she felt a tinge of doubt. Right now, nothing about Impala added up. The mare seemed totally sweet and relaxed. "What is it about you that goes wrong on the field, huh?" she murmured. As she continued to sweep the mitt over Impala, the mare sighed and half closed her eyes. Amy covered every inch of her, watching to see if Impala was ticklish anywhere. The mare remained in a half doze until she finished. She became more alert when Amy slid her saddle on but didn't object, even when her girth was tightened. Impala opened her mouth for the snaffle bit and stayed still as Amy did up the noseband and throatlatch. She checked the girth again and looped her reins over the pony's head. "Walk on."

Impala nudged Amy's shoulder before walking calmly out of her stall, up the aisle, and onto the yard. Amy pulled her stirrups down and swung onto the mare's back. Alfredo led Archie out a few moments later. He checked his girth before mounting. The bay gelding struck the ground with his hoof, and Amy smiled. It was as if Archie were inviting her to admire his new shoe.

"Let's go," Alfredo said, shortening his reins. He guided Archie down toward the redbrick arch. The bay arched his muscular neck, and Alfredo leaned forward to give him a quick pat.

Amy nudged Impala with her heels, and the mare moved forward. She settled into the mare's stride as they rode under the archway and down the path. Alfredo turned right onto a broad grassy track that ran alongside the paddocks. Two foals chased each other around an elm tree while their mothers dozed. Amy wondered how they found the energy to run when it was so hot. Even though it was late afternoon, the heat still shimmered up from the ground.

She patted Impala's shoulder. The mare walked rapidly, her stride long and fast. Amy was reminded of her horse, Spindleberry, and the way his long limbs flew so smoothly across the ground. He was nearly a whole hand taller than Impala but, like her, he was narrow and finely built. Impala arched her neck and shortened her stride as they rode down the track. Amy closed her fingers on the reins, sensing that the mare was about to break into a trot.

Alfredo glanced back. "Are you ready to up the pace?"

"Even if I'm not, Impala sure is," Amy replied with a grin. She shortened her reins and sat deep in the saddle. Impala tossed her head and immediately broke into a canter. "Hey, where are you going, Speedy Gonzales?" She closed her legs and tightened her fingers on the reins, and Impala returned to a trot. "She responds to the lightest touch," Amy commented enthusiastically. "You trained her really well."

Alfredo half halted Archie so he could ride alongside Amy and Impala. "She's got the potential to be amazing on the field. She's fast off the mark and can turn on a dime."

She focused on Impala's stride. "I get the feeling that she loves to please but at the same time she's raring to go."

Alfredo nodded. "That pretty much sums her up. I just don't understand why she decides to freak out on the polo pitch."

Archie's pace matched Impala's as they turned onto a narrow path that led to a grove. They slowed to a walk, and Alfredo began to talk about his family. "I'm sorry Papa was so blunt earlier. I'd like to say it's age, but he's always been like that!"

"It's OK. He's not the first person to be suspicious of alternative methods," Amy reassured him.

"It's crazy, really, because he — more than anyone — should be open to something different. His father grew up on the family ranch in Argentina raising cattle, and when he took over the farm, he sold most of the cattle and turned his attention to breeding Criollo horses. When Papa made the decision to buy Manticore and breed him with the best of his father's horses, everyone thought they were out of their minds for turning their backs on the family cattle business, but Papa refused to listen."

"When did your family make the move from Argentina?" Amy asked.

"Papa bought this estate after he had a few successful polo seasons," Alfredo replied. "This was a better place to be because we were closer to the North American polo circuit. But he never sold the ranch. He put a foreman there and it's used for rearing cattle again."

That sounds a lot like Mom, Amy thought. *She began Heartland on nothing more than a wing and a prayer. But she was so determined so dedicated that she succeeded where others only saw failure.*

"Are you OK to gallop?" Alfredo asked. There was an open field beyond the grove that was flat and inviting.

Amy felt a rush of enthusiasm. "You bet!"

Impala picked up on Amy's anticipation and began to prance. Amy waited for Archie to go first and held Impala back for a moment. The mare obeyed but tugged against the reins, telling Amy that she wanted to run, too. She gave Impala her head and let out a whoop of joy as the mare plunged forward. In seconds, Impala was galloping full out, her hooves drumming over the ground in a sweet rhythm. "Go, beautiful, go!" Amy murmured as she crouched close to Impala's neck. The ground was just a blur as they inched closer to Archie.

Alfredo glanced over his shoulder, his face registering surprise as Impala edged up so her nose was level with

Archie's quarters. "Come on, Arch, you can't let a couple of girls beat us!" he teased.

"Did you hear that?" Amy called to Impala. The mare's ears flicked back. "It's time to put the boys in their place!" She closed her legs tighter against Impala's sides, and the mare put on another burst of speed.

Impala snorted as she drew neck and neck with Archie. But as the fence at the edge of the field came closer, Amy reluctantly slowed the mare. "Whoa, Impala." The pony pulled against her hands, but Amy kept up a firm pressure until the mare slowed to a halt.

She stared after Alfredo, who kept up his breakneck pace. *He'll crash right through — there's no way Archie will clear it at that speed*, she thought. Amy's heart began to thud.

Impala seemed to feel Amy's tension and started to dance on the spot. Just when Amy was convinced she was about to see a collision, Alfredo pulled Archie up, standing up in the stirrups and closing his hands on the reins. The bay's muscles strained to obey Alfredo's signal, and in a few short strides he came to an abrupt halt.

Impala tossed her head and pawed the ground. "I'm sorry, girl," Amy said, patting her shoulder. "You knew you had plenty of time to stop. I'm a rookie when it comes to what a polo pony can and can't do."

"One for the boys!" Alfredo was grinning widely as he cantered back.

"We let you win, in case you didn't notice," Amy shot back with a playful smile.

"Yeah, right." Alfredo raised his eyebrows. "Wasn't that you screaming at Impala to beat us?"

Amy took a pretend swipe at him as he came alongside her. "I don't scream at horses. You're just not familiar with giving clear instructions."

Alfredo laughed. "I have a feeling you're going to get along very well with Susannah and my sisters," he told Amy.

They rode through an open gateway in a corner of the field. The trail wound its way down to a creek. The relief from the sun as they rode under the trees was instantaneous. Impala waded into the shallow water and dropped her head to drink. Amy let the reins slip through her fingers to allow Impala the freedom to stretch her neck. It was getting increasingly hard to remember that she had come to the Hamptons to work with the mare because there were problems with her behavior.

Alfredo glanced across at her. "You're probably wondering what the difficulty is with Impala."

"She's your horse and if you say she has a problem, then I believe you," Amy said.

"You need to see her in a polo game. She becomes a totally different horse. We're playing the day after tomorrow, so you'll be able to see her in action then." Alfredo pulled up Archie's head and rode him toward the opposite bank.

Amy gathered her reins but let Impala find her own way over the stony bed. With a splash, the mare jumped up onto the bank and followed Archie along a narrow, winding track. Amy settled back into the pony's stride and continued to puzzle over how a horse with her sweet, willing nature could change personalities so drastically.

Without warning, Impala shied, springing sideways across the track with a clatter of hooves. Amy lost one stirrup and only kept her seat by grabbing a handful of Impala's mane. "Steady," she called, looking to see what had spooked the pony.

Impala was eyeing a tree stump at the edge of the track. "Do you think it's a monster?" Amy asked in a soothing voice as she stroked her neck. She took back her stirrup and tightened her legs around Impala. "Come on, I won't let anything get you." She kept her legs firmly on the girth to encourage Impala to keep moving and continued to talk to the mare in a cheerful voice.

Alfredo glanced back. "Are you OK?"

"Fine, thanks," Amy called back. "Impala doesn't like the tree stump."

"She sometimes spooks at things," Alfredo said. "Sorry, I should have warned you."

Amy leaned forward to pat Impala's neck as the mare sidled past the stump, watching it from the corner of her eye as they passed. "You're kind of a baby, aren't you?"

On the way home, she watched out for anything else that might spook Impala, but the mare remained calm. As soon as they clattered onto the yard, Chrissie the stable hand walked up.

She smiled up at Amy. "How'd she do?"

"Really well," Amy said as she dropped her stirrups and swung to the ground.

Chrissie took Impala's and Archie's reins and led them away. Amy stared after the horses. She'd wanted to rub Impala down and give her a small feed as a thank-you for the ride.

"Feel like swimming before dinner?" Alfredo asked.

"Sure." But as she headed back to the house, Amy still wasn't comfortable about handing Impala off to someone else at the end of her ride. Her mother had told her over and over, *Always see to your horse's needs before your own.* Even though she knew that Impala would be receiving the best of care, she still wanted to be the one to untack the mare and get her settled. Again she compared the Escobar way of doing things with how they did things at Heartland. She knew that even if they could afford a hundred hands on staff, she'd never want to hand over Sundance or Spindle to a groom at the end of a ride.

"Is five minutes enough time for you to get changed?" Alfredo asked as the house came into sight.

"I'll race you," Amy challenged, reminding herself that this wasn't her home, and she wasn't here to criticize the way the Escobars kept their horses — which was fault-less as far as their welfare was concerned. "And this time I'm not going to lose!"

She slipped off her riding clothes and took a quick shower before getting into her bathing suit. When she was ready, she realized that she'd taken closer to fifteen minutes than five. But as she left her room she saw Alfredo heading up the corridor in a short navy bathrobe.

"Do you still want to race?" he teased.

"I would, but I'm not sure where the pool is," Amy admitted.

Alfredo laughed and Amy felt butterflies stirring in her stomach again.

From the hall, Alfredo led the way out of the house. As Amy stepped onto the sun terrace, she saw the pool a short distance away in the yard. Two girls were al-ready in the water playing with an inflatable ball. A net was stretched out between them. The girls both had the same dark hair and eyes and olive skin as Al-fredo. Sounds of laughter and splashing made their way up to the house.

The girls stopped and the girl facing them waved. "Alfredo! Come and play!"

A fence surrounded the pool, and Alfredo held open the gate for Amy to enter. "These are my sisters, Dacil and Celeste," Alfredo told Amy, gesturing to the girls as he named them. "I mentioned them earlier."

"Oh, you don't want to listen to anything Alfredo says about us, Amy," one of the girls said as she swam over to the edge of the pool. "We didn't pay any attention to the stuff he told us about you!" Her dark eyes danced with mischief. "Alfredo, I want Amy on my side. You get to play with Dacil."

"Fine with me," Amy said as she slipped off the sarong she was using as a cover-up and laid it over one of the recliners. She wondered exactly what Alfredo had said about her to his sisters.

"See if you feel that way after you've seen Celeste hit the ball." Dacil giggled and ducked as Celeste smacked the surface and sent a spray of water at her.

Amy sat on the side of the pool before jumping into the water. She sighed as she felt the coolness of the water wash over her, and flipped to float on her back.

Out of the corner of her, eye she saw Alfredo take off his robe and walk to the deep end of the pool. Alfredo raised his arms and made a perfect dive into the water. *Pretty good,* Amy thought as he swam underwater and resurfaced by the net in the middle of the pool.

"Mom said that Alfredo took you down to the barn. Did he show you my pony?" Celeste asked.

Amy shook her head.

Celeste tossed her long black braid over her back. "Her name's Minerva. She's an Appaloosa, so you can't miss her. She won all of her jumping classes this year."

"That's fantastic," Amy said. "So you're not into polo?"

"It's OK, I guess," Celeste said casually, "but Dacil and I prefer show jumping. I applied to take Minerva away with me when I begin high school next year."

"When you've finished interviewing Amy, maybe we can start the game?" Alfredo called as he tossed the ball into the air.

Celeste rolled her eyes at Amy.

"What school did you apply to?" Amy asked as they swam closer to the net.

"Chestnut Hill," Celeste told her. "Do you know it?"

"Sure," Amy said, thinking back on her visit to the school. "I wish I could have gone there. The riding program is great."

"Do you know the school?" Dacil asked with curiosity.

"I gave a symposium there on complementary medicine, and I helped one of the ponies who was having a few problems," Amy told her.

"Like you're going to do with Impala," Dacil said.

Amy didn't have time to answer because at that moment Alfredo sent the ball flying across the net. She dove for it and slapped it back in a spray of water. Alfredo jumped to hit the ball again and then yelled as he disappeared under the water. Celeste had grabbed his legs and dragged him under.

By the time he had resurfaced, spluttering, Celeste had swum back under the net and appeared beside Amy.

"No fair!" Dacil yelled.

Celeste ignored her and grinned at Amy. "First point to us. This is going to be an easy victory!"

❧

Amy sat at the dressing table in her room and glanced at her watch. It was six-thirty and dinner was at seven. There was just enough time to e-mail Soraya, her best friend. She was on vacation in the Florida Keys with her boyfriend, Anthony.

Amy got set up at her laptop and quickly began typing.

Hey, Soraya,

It's amazing here! It's five-star service everywhere — even down on the stable yard. I'll have to try not to get used to it!

Impala's really sweet and we had a great ride today. I think Alfredo's worried that I don't believe him about her behavior. I can tell that he's really anxious about her.

Amy paused. She knew that her friend would be really interested in how well she was getting to know Alfredo.

She was tempted to tell her exactly how good-looking he was, but she didn't want Soraya to get too excited about a possible summer romance for Amy. While she was here she had to concentrate on the task at hand.

> It's good that Alfredo's so focused on working with Impala. But we had a lot of fun today riding and swimming in his pool. I'm headed down for dinner but I'll write again soon.
> XOXO
> Amy

Amy hit SEND and stood up to check herself in the mirror. She wanted to look nice for her first dinner with the Escobars and had put on her favorite blue dress, which had a sweetheart neckline.

It was five to seven, so she quickly applied some lip gloss and headed out of the room. As she switched off the light, she wondered if Alfredo would notice her outfit. She knew her visit was all about Impala, but she couldn't help hoping that Alfredo's dark eyes would light up when she walked into the room.

Chapter Five

❧

Amy took some time to check out the family portraits as she made her way downstairs. The Escobar men all had the same large dark eyes, thick black hair, and strong jawlines. A portrait of a woman with graying hair pulled back in a bun was hung alongside Papa's. *She must be his late wife,* Amy thought, noting the warmth in the woman's eyes despite her stern expression. The next portraits were of Juan and his wife and then Pablo and Susannah. Amy frowned. There didn't seem to be a portrait of Alfredo's mother. Maybe it was out of sensitivity to Susannah. *But I haven't seen images of Alfredo's mom anywhere in the house,* she thought. There were plenty of photos of the men playing polo and of the family on vacation on palm-edged tropical beaches, or on safari in Africa. Amy frowned. Susannah didn't seem the type to refuse to have pictures of Pablo's first wife around, so why weren't there any?

She continued down the stairs and found Susannah standing in the hallway putting on a linen jacket. "There's been a sudden change of plans," she said when she saw Amy. "We're taking you out for a sunset picnic. I hope you're not too disappointed that we're not staying in for dinner."

"A picnic sounds wonderful," Amy responded. She glanced down at her dress. "But I might be overdressed. Let me just run and change."

"I'll wait for you in the car," Susannah told her.

Amy hurried back to her room. *I guess the dress will have to wait*, she mused as she changed into white capris and a striped T-shirt.

Susannah smiled as Amy climbed into the back of the chauffeured limousine. "Very nautical. You must have read our minds."

Amy glanced at Dacil and Celeste on the opposite seat. "Are we going rowing?" she asked as she looked over the girls' casual outfits.

Dacil wrinkled her nose. "That's too much like work," she said, and then laughed.

"We thought we'd take a sunset sail on Alfredo's boat," Susannah explained. "I asked Mrs. Willson, our cook, to put a picnic together for us. I'm afraid it was pretty short notice, so please don't expect anything too fancy."

"I bet Mrs. Willson will sulk for days now that you ruined Amy's welcome dinner," Celeste said with laughter in her eyes. "She'll probably make cold cabbage stew tomorrow night to get back at you."

"Celeste," Susannah said reprovingly.

Amy wondered why the family dinner had been canceled at the last minute. "Will Alfredo be joining us?" she asked, trying to sound unconcerned.

"He went ahead to get the boat ready," Susannah said. "Papa and Pablo had to go out. One of the neighboring stud farms is selling a horse that might be a suitable replacement for Elvira."

Amy felt a jolt of surprise that Alfredo hadn't gone, too. Wouldn't Papa and Pablo have wanted his opinion on whatever horse they were trying out? *Maybe he felt he couldn't go because it's my first night here,* she thought. Amy turned to stare out the window and felt uncomfortable. She hoped Alfredo knew that she would understand if he needed to attend to things for the team instead of taking care of her.

They drove down a street lined with old-fashioned lampposts, fancy shops, and restaurants. The stores were a world away from the ones in the malls Amy was used to shopping in. She glimpsed displays of pottery, jewelry, books, flowers, fishing tackle, wine, and antiques as they made their way down Main Street. They drove out of town and a little while later pulled into a parking lot near a small marina.

Strains of classical music drifted on the breeze from a concert being held in a nearby park. It was almost as though Amy had stepped into a different time.

Dacil and Celeste ran across to the harbor and pounded along the boarded dock.

"Amy and I can carry this," Susannah told the driver as he lifted a small cooler out of the trunk. "I'll call when we're ready to be picked up."

"Have a nice evening," the chauffeur replied with a small nod and touch of his cap.

As they walked toward the rows of boats, Amy said hesitantly, "I wouldn't have minded Alfredo going to see the pony with Papa and Pablo."

Susannah's pace slowed. "That's sweet of you, but," she hesitated, "Papa and Pablo took off without inviting Alfredo."

Amy blinked. "Oh."

Susannah sighed. "Pablo thought that it was more important that Alfredo stay at home on your first night, but I'm afraid Alfredo's reading more than that into the decision. The Escobar men aren't known for their communication skills!" she added playfully.

Amy felt her stomach churn in anticipation of Alfredo's

response to being left behind by the other men. She hoped he was taking it better than she feared.

Susannah put down the cooler and turned to face Amy. "I'm telling you this not because I want you to feel at all awkward, but so you can understand if Alfredo's not quite himself this evening."

Thinking of how charming Alfredo had been earlier that day, Amy couldn't imagine him letting his hurt show. Then she noted the look in Susannah's dark eyes and realized how concerned she was about her stepson. "Thanks for warning me," Amy said.

"He's not finding things easy at the moment," Susannah said. She looked as if she might say more but then picked up the cooler again. "Anyway," her tone was brighter, "Pablo and Papa rushing off made me think that we ought to get out, too."

"I'm glad." Amy gave Susannah's arm a quick squeeze. "It's lovely here."

"Wait until you get out on the boat," Susannah told her with a grin.

Alfredo's boat was docked alongside a much larger sailboat. Amy guessed that it belonged to the family as well, since the name *Escobar* was written in script on its side. Amy looked down the length of Alfredo's yacht, but its pristine white sides were clear of any name.

"Does Alfredo's boat have a name?" Amy asked as she checked out the smaller yacht.

"He's still trying to make up his mind what to call her," Susannah said. "Aren't you, Alfredo?"

At Susannah's call, Alfredo appeared at the side of the yacht and leaned over to take the cooler from her. He placed it on the deck and returned to offer a hand to Amy. Amy put her fingers into his strong grip and stepped onboard. The boat rocked slightly and Amy stumbled. Immediately, Alfredo put his hand on her back to steady her. Amy felt a tingle shoot up her spine at his touch. "I've got it now, thanks," she said self-consciously.

Susannah stepped onto the deck next to Amy and led her toward the leather seats at the far end of the boat.

"Come and sit by me, Amy," Celeste called, and patted the space beside her.

Amy glanced over her shoulder. "Does Alfredo need a hand sailing?"

"He's fine," Susannah said. "These motorized sailboats are really easy to sail."

"You didn't say that when you nearly crashed into the dock last week," Dacil said, chuckling.

Susannah tipped back her head and gave a low laugh. "Oh, Amy, I can never have any secrets with my daughters around!"

Amy sat down and watched Alfredo move quickly and efficiently around the deck, coiling the mooring rope before climbing up a short ladder to sit behind the wheel.

The engine whirred, and the sailboat pulled slowly away from the harbor and into the open sea. A flock of gulls rose up into the sky with indignant cries as the vessel cut through the water. Amy breathed in the salty air and gave a contented sigh. This was a perfect way to end the day.

Alfredo followed the coastline past enormous mansions and private docks until a beautiful beach with white sand came into sight. As they drew nearer to the shore, two Jet Skis roared past, leaving a foamy trail behind in the water.

Alfredo cut the engines. "This is as close as I can get without running aground," he called.

Susannah and the girls stood up and walked over to the edge of the deck. Amy leaned over the rail and saw, attached to the boat, a ladder that led down to a large dinghy.

Alfredo climbed down first with the cooler under one arm and waited for the others to join him. Amy followed down and settled herself onto one of the wooden seats. Once everyone was seated, Alfredo untied the dinghy from the yacht and picked up the oars.

Amy trailed her fingers in the cool water as Alfredo rowed them to the beach. His fitness from playing polo allowed him to move the oars with ease, and they reached the shore in no time. Alfredo climbed out and into the shallow water, pulling the dinghy behind him. Amy quickly pulled off her running shoes and jumped out to help.

"Thanks," Alfredo said as they grounded the boat on the dry sand.

"Sure," Amy said. But before she could say another word, Alfredo lifted the cooler out of the boat and strode up the beach. He seemed like a different person from the one Amy had gone trail riding with earlier in the day. Her heart sank as she wondered if Alfredo's mood was entirely due to Papa and Pablo's actions. She understood that he'd be upset, but it was surprising that he was acting so aloof. Amy hated the idea that Alfredo's mood was going to ruin Susannah's sunset picnic.

Susannah, Dacil, and Celeste's chatter distracted Amy from Alfredo's silence as they sat down on the picnic blanket. But as they began to set out the food for dinner, Amy suddenly felt self-conscious. *I guess he's disappointed to be stuck here entertaining me,* she thought.

She brought her attention back to the picnic, determined to enjoy herself. Susannah passed her a rye cracker with dark jam spread on it. Amy eyed it warily for a second and then took a bite.

"Do you like it?" Dacil asked curiously. "I hate caviar."

Caviar?! Amy was used to peanut butter and jelly and cold cuts at a picnic.

"Please let Mrs. Willson have packed something edible," Dacil said as she rummaged through the cooler. "Yes!" She unwrapped a package of cold pizza slices. "Real food!"

Amy smiled and shook her head when Susannah offered her more caviar. "I'm afraid I'm with Dacil on this one," she apologized.

"Try some goat cheese and caramelized onion instead," Susannah said, handing her a crusty baguette. "It's one of my favorite combinations."

Amy bit into the sandwich and smiled. "*This* is right up my alley. Thanks."

Alfredo helped himself to some smoked salmon on crackers and stared out to sea, his face expressionless.

"You know how you said that you've been to Chestnut Hill? Did you get together with any of the riders on the junior jumping team?" Celeste asked Amy. "I'm planning to try out."

"Chestnut Hill is all she ever talks about. Mom, can't you get her to talk about something else?" Dacil quipped.

"Sorry, hon, but the last time I checked, your sister had a mind of her own," Susannah replied, her eyes bright with amusement.

"I got to know Malory O'Neil pretty well," Amy admitted. "She rides Tybalt, the horse I mentioned helping earlier."

Celeste frowned. "They've got a problem horse on the team?"

"I'm losing the will . . . to eat. . . ." Dacil rolled her eyes upward and collapsed onto her side in the sand.

"He's actually an amazing show jumper but he needed to work through some emotional issues when he first arrived at the school," Amy told Celeste.

"Like Impala." Dacil sat back up.

"Maybe," Amy said carefully, aware that Alfredo might be listening.

"Have you come across many horses like Impala?" Susannah asked as she handed out bottles of mineral water.

"Every case is unique," Amy replied. "But I have worked with lots of horses who, like Impala, have great dispositions most of the time but for some reason end up acting totally out of character. I try to find out what's causing that difference and then work on building up their trust and confidence."

"Well, we're thrilled you came to work with Impala," Susannah said. "Aren't we, Alfredo?"

"Huh?" Alfredo looked distracted.

"I was saying how happy we are that Amy's come to help Impala," Susannah repeated.

"Yes." Alfredo nodded. "Sure."

The sun had begun to disappear below the horizon,

and the sky was turning brilliant shades of pink and purple.

Susannah glanced at her watch and fished her cell phone out of her pocket. "It's getting late. Would you mind if I get the car to drive around and pick up the girls and me instead of returning on the boat with you and Alfredo?"

"Mom!" Dacil protested. "I want to stay with Amy and Alfredo."

"Not tonight, sweetheart," Susannah replied. "You need to get home and get ready for bed."

With a mutinous expression, Dacil tossed her long dark hair over her shoulder. She began to draw patterns in the sand with her finger.

Susannah called the driver and then began to pack the dishes and containers away. Amy collected the empty water bottles and placed them in the cooler. She half wished she could go back in the car, too. Alfredo was making it clear that he was in no mood for company.

Susannah stood up and brushed the sand off her pants. "By the time we walk up to the road, the car should be here. Enjoy the rest of the evening, you two."

"Right," Alfredo said.

"Thanks for the picnic," Amy added. She waved good-bye to Celeste and Dacil, who were lagging behind Susannah as they walked up the beach toward the road.

Amy turned to watch two surfers down the shore as they ran to the water. They splashed as they plopped onto their boards and paddled out to catch the bigger waves. The sun was gone now and the sky was quickly getting dark. As the silence stretched between Amy and Alfredo, she felt irritated again. *I guess he's not the guy I thought he was,* she mused.

"I'm not exactly great company tonight, am I?" Alfredo suddenly said.

Amy hesitated. "You've obviously got a lot on your mind."

Alfredo nodded. "True. But I hope I haven't ruined tonight for you."

Amy sighed. "Do you want to talk?" she offered tentatively.

Alfredo looked surprised. He ran his hand over his hair and said, "You don't mind me unloading on you?"

"Come on," Amy said as she stood up. "We can walk at the same time."

They walked over the firm sand in silence for a while. Every so often Alfredo stooped down to pick up a pebble or shell. He threw one of the pebbles and it skipped a few times over the water before sinking. "I don't know if Susannah told you, but Papa and Dad went to look at a horse tonight," he said.

Amy nodded. "She mentioned it."

"I know they've had doubts about me ever since Impala started misbehaving, but I didn't realize how serious it was until tonight. It's obvious that they don't trust my judgment. I've always been involved in decisions affecting the team. Leaving me out is as good as telling me I'm on probation." Alfredo's voice sounded raw.

Amy shook her head. "I think you're reading too much into it. Your dad and grandfather probably didn't think past the fact that it's my first night here as your guest and it would be wrong to leave me on my own."

Alfredo considered that for a moment. "I hadn't looked at it that way," he admitted. "But if they really wanted my opinion, they could have gone to look at the mare in the morning."

"I'm sure that if they like the horse, they'll go back with you before making a final decision." She hesitated. "I don't think jumping to conclusions about your position on the team is a good idea. Impala needs you to be positive and focused on her." She spoke gently, hoping Alfredo would understand that she wasn't trying to lecture him.

Alfredo shrugged. "I guess you're right." He chuckled. "I should have talked this through with you a couple of hours ago!"

"Well, you had no way of knowing the depths of my

wisdom," Amy said, keeping her expression totally straight. A moment later she squealed with laughter as Alfredo kicked water at her. She splashed him back and then agreed to a truce.

As they walked side by side back to the dinghy, Amy thought what an intriguing person Alfredo was. He was determined to do everything possible to help Impala, but at the same time he didn't have any confidence in himself. She glanced at his handsome profile against the gathering dusk and realized how attracted to him she was. Even though they weren't touching, it felt like there was electricity sparking between them; she was acutely aware of how close his hand was to hers. Being with Alfredo was comfortable and exciting at the same time.

She wanted to reach out and touch him now that they had broken through the wall he'd held between them all night. But she made herself hold back. She knew getting involved with Alfredo was wrong. *I need to focus on Impala. I came out here to help her and I can't let anything or anyone — even Alfredo — distract me from that.*

Chapter Six

❧

Amy awoke to the distant sound of a horse whinnying. She sat up in bed, panicking that she'd overslept. *I'll be late for my riding class,* she thought frantically. She looked around and tried to remember which student she was supposed to be teaching and it dawned on her: She wasn't at Sal's, she was in the Hamptons.

She glanced at the clock on her bedside table and noticed with a start that it was twenty past eight. She'd gone to sleep without setting an alarm, assuming that she'd wake up early as usual. But being in such a comfortable bed had taken a toll: She'd slept for nine hours straight!

Amy hopped out of bed and pulled on her yard clothes. She guessed that Alfredo would already be down at the barn seeing to his horses. She ran down the sweeping staircase and burst into the kitchen.

"Hey, Amy." Alfredo looked up from his newspaper as she hurried into the room. "How did you sleep?"

Amy blinked in surprise to see him still at the table. "Too well! I slept way past my usual time."

"Everyone else has eaten, but help yourself." Alfredo nodded at a series of silver hot plates on the sideboard. "Do you want coffee?" He reached for the pot.

"That sounds perfect," Amy said as she helped herself to scrambled eggs, home fries, bacon, and toast. She pulled out the chair opposite Alfredo. *Chrissie must see to Alfredo's horses each morning,* she realized.

Alfredo poured her coffee. "Are you OK to head down to the yard on your own after you eat? I usually like to get out there before it gets too hot."

"Sure." Amy nodded. "So what's a typical training session like?" She took a sip of her coffee.

"Today we're doing a stick-and-ball session in the outdoor arena. It's basically practicing chasing and hitting the ball," Alfredo added when he saw Amy's blank expression.

As she ate her breakfast, Amy considered just how much she had to learn about polo. Not knowing what made a polo pony tick might result in missing out on a vital clue to Impala's behavior. Fortunately, Alfredo seemed totally focused on working with the mare today, and that would help Amy's concentration. The electricity she'd felt walking along the beach last night seemed to have vanished. In fact, when she thought back on the evening, she realized it had faded as soon as they reached the boat. Alfredo had been absorbed in getting them back to the marina and Amy had spent the ride back alone, gazing up at the starry sky. But she couldn't forget walking beside him along the sand and hearing him laugh softly. *Enough!* she told herself firmly. *That's not why you're here!*

Once she finished her breakfast, Amy walked down to the yard. She found Alfredo talking to one of the stable hands, Helen, who was leading a gray mare with a foal at foot. "Is my father around?"

"No." The girl halted the mare. "He went down to the arena about ten minutes ago."

"Can you tell Chrissie to get Archie and Impala ready and bring them down to us?" Alfredo asked.

"No problem," Helen called back as she walked off.

"I'll tell her," Amy offered. "I want to have a quick word with her about Impala's stable routine. I'll catch up with you in a few minutes."

"OK," Alfredo said. "I'll see you down at the arena."

Amy found Chrissie grooming Archie. "Good morning," she said over the stall door.

Chrissie looked up and pushed a strand of long, dark hair away from her face. "Hi."

Amy took a deep breath, suddenly feeling awkward. Chrissie obviously knew her job inside out, and the last thing Amy wanted to do was to make her feel as though Amy blamed her for Impala's behavior. "Alfredo said that you see to Impala's stable routine. I was wondering if you'd mind talking me through it. I'm trying to build up a picture of her. She's a bit of a mystery at the moment."

"Other than what happens on the polo field, what you see is what you get," Chrissie said as she drew a body brush over Archie's already gleaming coat. "I'd say she's got the sweetest nature of the entire team. She loves to please. That's why none of us can figure out why she goes so nuts during a match."

"What's her diet?" Amy asked.

"All of her feed's been overseen by a nutritionist to check that the nutritional and caloric content are OK." Chrissie cleaned the body brush against a curry comb and switched to Archie's other side. "Her routine at the moment is to come in at six A.M. for a small feed. Then I groom her and pick out her feet. If Alfredo's training her, I tack her up at nine. She has another small meal in the afternoon, and I quarter her before turning her out between four and six, depending on how hot it is."

Amy nodded. Impala's routine was designed to keep her settled and calm, with a steady intake of energy throughout the day to fuel her activity. "And there's no history that might help? Alfredo said that she's homebred."

Chrissie smiled. "I was there for her birth. It was amazing, especially seeing the instant bond between Impala and her dam, Blossom. Alfredo played classical music in the stable. He was so excited that she was going to be his first horse to train completely on his own. He wanted to be there right from her first moment."

Amy was touched by Chrissie's description of Alfredo's dedication. "Thanks for sharing all that with me," she said. "There really don't seem to be any clues as to what's triggering Impala's bad behavior."

Chrissie straightened up. "Don't take this the wrong way. I mean, if you can find something that the rest of us have missed, then I'll be as happy as anyone. But if you're looking for some obvious cause for Impala's behavior, then you're out of luck." She shrugged. "Maybe she's just trying to tell us that she doesn't enjoy polo."

She's sure trying to tell us something, Amy thought. But with Impala's breeding and training, it didn't make sense that she didn't enjoy the sport.

"Alfredo would like Archie and Impala tacked up," Amy remembered to say. "Shall I do Impala?"

"No thanks, I'll get them," Chrissie told her.

Amy took a quick peek into Impala's stall. The mare was pulling at her hayrack and she looked at Amy with a calm expression in her dark brown eyes. "I'll see you soon," Amy told her.

She left the stable yard and hurried past the yearlings' barn and the stallions' stables. She headed under a red-brick arch onto the same path where she had met Pablo the previous day. The path opened onto a yard that housed a large glass building. *The horse pool,* Amy guessed. Opposite the pool was an indoor arena and straight ahead was the outdoor arena from which she could hear the thudding of hooves. Alfredo was sitting on the top bar of the gate with his back to her.

As Amy drew closer, she could see Pablo galloping up the center of the arena on a black gelding.

"That's Wayward, one of our youngsters," Alfredo explained as Amy joined him at the gate. "He's a year younger than Impala, but he's way more mature on the pitch."

The arena was larger than standard, to give the horses enough room to gallop and turn. Pablo swung his polo mallet down and leaned out of the saddle as his horse neared the ball. There was a loud crack as the mallet made contact with the solid plastic ball. It soared through the air and landed at the far end of the arena. Pablo straightened up and urged his horse to go faster. The pair galloped toward the fence at breakneck speed but then Pablo shortened Wayward's stride and turned a tight circle around the ball. He hit the ball once more and it traveled half the length of the arena.

"Nice job!" Amy cheered, clapping. Pablo glanced over, swung his mallet up onto his shoulder, and cantered over.

"Morning," Pablo said with a smile. "What do you think of him?" He leaned forward to pat Wayward's neck.

"You've got a great partnership," Amy said, appreciating how in tune the two had been in their pursuit of the ball.

Pablo nodded. "Polo is all about teamwork. There's your relationship with your fellow players, your relationship with your horse, and your horse's relationship with you."

Now he's talking my language, Amy thought.

She turned at the sound of horses' hooves. Chrissie was leading Impala and Archie toward them.

"Ah, Chrissie. Take Wayward back to the yard for me, please," Pablo said, jumping down from the gelding. "And could you ask Helen to bring down Lily?" He winked at Amy. "Now's your chance to get into polo as much as we are!"

Amy smiled and took Archie's reins. "Do you mind if I watch you on Impala?" she asked Alfredo. "I'd like to see how she does for you."

He nodded. "Here." He handed her a hat. "I brought this down for you."

Amy took the polo hat with its bill that almost circled

the helmet. She buckled it on and checked Archie's girth before mounting. Chrissie opened the arena gate so Amy and Alfredo could ride in and then took Wayward from Pablo and led him out of the arena. "Good luck," she called over her shoulder as she returned to the stables.

Amy raised her hand and then pushed Archie into a trot. The saddle was specially designed for polo playing and its design felt strange.

She circled the arena to warm up the gelding. Just like Impala's, his stride felt long, even though he was barely over fifteen hands tall. Although he wasn't pulling on the Pelham bit's double reins, Amy could feel the energy in his strong hindquarters. The Pelham bit allowed all that power to be controlled by the lightest touch on the reins. She glanced at Impala, who was trotting calmly for Alfredo on the opposite side of the arena. Alfredo had her working on the bit, her neck arched and her stride balanced.

Amy finished her warm-up and went to get a mallet from Pablo. She transferred the two sets of reins into one hand.

"Archie will respond to the reins on his neck like so," Pablo said, flattening the double reins against the gelding's neck to demonstrate. "All polo ponies are trained to obey neck-reining signals."

Amy nodded and took the mallet from Pablo. It felt

lighter than it looked but as soon as she began to trot, she felt off balance. She took a practice swing and came nowhere near the ground. Glancing down, she realized she would have to lean way out of the saddle to be able to hit the ball.

Amy swung again and felt herself slipping as she was pulled to one side. She swung the mallet up into the air to help regain her balance.

"This time, try to swing at the ball," Pablo called, tossing it into the middle of the ring. When Amy turned Archie at the ball, the gelding swung around so sharply that she thought for one moment his legs would go out from under him. She kept her inside leg on the girth and her outside leg farther back for balance, but Archie surged forward and his canter became a gallop as he raced at the ball. Amy's mind was racing. *Steady, Archie, you might know what you're doing, but I'm a rookie!*

She squeezed her legs to bring Archie onto the bit and then pulled back with the reins to slow the gelding. Archie responded reluctantly, and Amy focused on the ball. She brought down her mallet and, bending at the waist, she leaned over to take a swipe at the ball. She swung wide to avoid hitting Archie's legs.

"Try again," Pablo shouted.

Amy turned Archie again, this time ready for the horse's sharp response. He reminded her of Loup, the mustang she had ridden on a cattle drive in Arizona.

Out of the corner of her eye she saw Alfredo cantering up alongside them.

"You swung too wide and too high," he told her. "Loosen up, feel like you're a piece of Jell-O. If the plate is shaken, the Jell-O moves, but its base always stays put!"

Amy forced herself to relax all over.

"Nice and easy, line up your shot. Stop Archie from falling out with your outside leg but keep your eye on the ball. Now, swing!"

Amy's mallet made contact with the ball and the impact reverberated through her arm. She nearly dropped the mallet but managed to haul it up while grabbing a section of Archie's mane with her other hand.

"A hit! Yeah!" Alfredo whooped.

Amy looked to see where the ball had landed. She spotted it only a few yards away in the sand. "Show me what you do," she said to Alfredo. She wanted to watch how he did it with Impala. She cantered Archie over to the fence and reined him around.

Alfredo cantered Impala past the ball and turned her on her haunches, sending a spray of sand up into the air. In one smooth motion, he leaned out of the saddle and whacked the ball. It flew into the air and landed at the other end of the arena. He urged Impala forward and the mare responded by stretching out her neck and galloping down to the ball.

Amy drew a deep breath as Alfredo continued past the ball and, in a skillful move, swung the mallet backward to send the ball scudding down the arena. He then spun Impala around and galloped after the ball once again.

Archie pawed at the ground, anxious to join in. "Steady," Amy murmured, without taking her eyes off Alfredo and Impala. The mare wasn't showing any signs of stress.

Archie turned to look at the gate and let out a piercing whinny. Pablo, mounted on Lily, a gray horse, was riding into the arena. He cantered at the ball at the same time as Alfredo was approaching from the opposite end of the arena on Impala.

Amy frowned. Suddenly, there was something wrong with Impala's stride. She wasn't focused on the ball but on resisting Alfredo's hands and legs. Her muscles were bunched and her stride uneven. Alfredo made a valiant swing at the ball just before Pablo reached it. But Impala swerved away and Alfredo missed by inches, almost falling off in the process.

Pablo hit the ball and called back over his shoulder. "Come on, Alfredo. Ride!"

Alfredo reined Impala around and set her in pursuit of the ball again. Impala responded by racing forward, her tail streaming like a banner. But the moment she neared Pablo and Lily, she threw up her head. Alfredo swung at the ball and missed as Impala shied away from the mallet. He turned the mare in a tight circle and chased after the ball that Pablo had hit back down the arena. With their head start, Impala and Alfredo reached the ball first, but as Alfredo swung his mallet forward, Impala plunged and bucked, nearly throwing him over her neck and into the sand. Lily and Pablo closed in to claim the ball while Alfredo grabbed a handful of Impala's mane in order to keep his seat.

Amy frowned as she watched Alfredo wheel Impala around and canter to the gate. The mare's tail was clamped down and the whites of her eyes were showing. Impala's behavior reminded her of Maverick, Cory Redpath's pony. The high-strung gelding had been stressed-out after being bullied by members of his herd. Could it be that Impala was being bullied by some of the other ponies? If she were, it would explain her reluctance to be on the pitch the moment another horse joined in the stick-and-ball game.

Amy scooped up her reins and cantered over to Alfredo. Alfredo's lips were set in a thin line. "Do you see what I mean now?"

Pablo cantered up on Lily, and Impala ran back a few steps. "What went wrong this time?"

Even though Pablo's tone was calm, Alfredo's cheeks turned red.

"Impala's behavior reminds me of another horse I worked with. I wonder if she's being bullied by any of the other horses. Would it be possible to keep her on her own for a while when they're turned out?" Amy spoke up before Alfredo had chance to respond.

Alfredo looked doubtful. "I've never seen any sign of her being picked on."

"She wasn't happy whenever Lily got close," Amy persisted. "She's showing signs of mistrust around other horses. She obviously doesn't like her personal space being invaded."

"But horses are herd animals. She needs the security of company when she's turned out," Pablo argued.

"True." Amy nodded. "But if she's being bullied, she's better away from them. The bullying might not be anything as obvious as being kicked or bitten. It could be psychological, like not allowing her to drink from the trough, or chasing her away from favorite grazing areas." She suddenly noticed Papa walking toward them from the direction of the house, leaning on his stick, and felt a prickle of nerves at the sight of him. "She could be turned out with another four-legged animal, like a cow or a goat, to give her company."

"It's worth a try, I guess," Pablo said. But Amy thought she heard uncertainty in his voice.

"Anything is worth a try," Alfredo agreed. He slipped down from Impala and ran his stirrups up.

Papa had gotten close enough to hear Amy's suggestion and made a snorting noise before speaking. "So, we bring you all the way out here and your great suggestion is that the horse should be separated from the others," Papa said, his tone incredulous. His bushy gray eyebrows furrowed. "You say that by separating her from the herd, she will suddenly undergo a miraculous transformation, no?"

Amy felt her cheeks begin to burn. "I'm not saying that. But it's something to try while I get to know Impala better."

"Pah!" Papa threw his hands up. "You think if one of our own horses was being bullied, we wouldn't know about it?" He turned and walked back across the yard.

"Forgive my father, Amy," Pablo apologized quickly. "We will, of course, be happy to try whatever you suggest."

As Amy reined Archie back so she could open the gate, she noticed the doubtful look that passed between Pablo and Alfredo. Her heart sank. It was clear that none of the Escobars had confidence in her suggestion. But right now she couldn't think of any other reason for Impala's baffling behavior. Alfredo was right: She really did turn into a different pony on the polo field.

Chapter Seven

Back at the yard, Chrissie took Impala from Alfredo. "Come on, girl, let's get you sponged down," she said.

Alfredo brushed dust off his breeches. "It's Ricardo's day off today, but I'll call him later to tell him your suggestion."

Amy nodded. "I'd also like to start treating Impala with some of the Bach Flower Remedies I brought with me. We use them in our work at Heartland. I'd like to give her larch for confidence, aspen for fear, and chestnut bud to help her break the cycle of negative behavior."

"OK. If you show them to Chrissie, she'll make sure Impala has them," Alfredo told her. He rubbed his hands over his face. "Do you think they'll make a difference?

I've never heard of them." There was a note of dejection in his voice.

"They'll definitely help," Amy replied as they began to walk back to the house. "Would you mind if I gave them to Impala myself? It might help me get to know her a little better."

Alfredo hesitated. "Can you keep Chrissie in the loop so she knows what's going on?"

"Sure," Amy agreed. She tried to keep her tone light as she went on, "I think it would be a good idea if you got involved in Impala's treatment, too. Maybe you could go down to the yard when Chrissie brings Impala in each morning and spend some time with her."

Alfredo remained silent for a moment. "I don't want to do anything to undermine Chrissie's position," he said at last. "She has a set routine, and while she might not object to you doing your stuff with Impala, if I suddenly start interfering, she might take it personally."

Amy suddenly felt a surge of frustration at the Escobars' setup. Everything clearly ran smoothly, but it was ridiculous that the routine couldn't be adapted when there was a need. She took a deep breath and tried to be tactful. "When we work with the horses at Heartland, spending quiet time with them is one of the most important parts of the healing process."

"I'm not saying there can be no quiet time." There was a hint of exasperation in Alfredo's voice. "I'm just saying that Chrissie is in charge of stable management, so this is something that needs to be dealt with between you and her."

Amy stopped abruptly, feeling a flash of anger flare up inside her. "Allowing flexibility into an established routine doesn't lessen professionalism in any way!" She turned on her heel and marched away.

"Amy!" Alfredo called after her, but Amy didn't turn back.

Heading back to the barn, she found Chrissie in the tack room. "Hey, would it be OK for me to take out one of the horses?" Amy made sure her tone was calm so Chrissie wouldn't detect how upset she was, but she definitely needed some time by herself.

"Sure. I haven't exercised Rufus today. Why don't you take him out?" Chrissie took down a saddle and bridle. "Do you want to ride in the arena or are you going out?"

"How far away is the beach?" Amy asked, suddenly longing for the freedom of a long gallop.

"A couple of miles. Ride down the main driveway and turn left. After about half a mile you'll see a bridle path on your right. That takes you down onto the beach," Chrissie told her. "Is Alfredo going with you?"

"Actually, I'm riding alone," Amy said as she took Rufus's tack from Chrissie. A break from Alfredo was just what she needed right now, before she said something she'd regret.

❧

"Easy, Rufus." Amy half halted the bright chestnut gelding. "Can you smell the sea air?" she asked, reaching forward to stroke his muscular neck.

Rufus snatched at the bit and extended his stride again. Amy remembered Alfredo telling her that he often had to hold Rufus back so he wouldn't run past the ball. She could feel the gelding's energy in his long, powerful stride. He was raring to go, but true to his training, he obeyed her signals to keep a slower pace. "As soon as we hit the beach you can run as much as you want, I promise," Amy said. She shortened the reins and allowed Rufus to extend his trot into a collected canter. The chestnut arched his neck as his hooves thudded along the dirt path.

Amy's thoughts returned to her conversation with Alfredo. *He must have known that I couldn't fix her right away. I don't have a magic wand,* she thought.

The path narrowed, and over the top of a hedge Amy could see a shimmering band of azure. She slowed Rufus to a walk as the trail peaked and then began to drop downhill. The sparkling blue water lay before her as far as she could see. The dirt path gave way to soft sand, and on either side of the trail grew short, rough-looking bushes. But all of a sudden the growth disappeared and they were riding out onto the open beach. Amy halted

Rufus. She breathed in the sea air and listened to the waves crashing over the sand. In the distance to her left, the beach was lined with sunbathers, but Amy turned Rufus in the opposite direction where the sand was empty. She shortened her stirrup leathers while Rufus pranced on the spot. "You'll get your run," she laughed. Leaning forward in the saddle she murmured, "OK, boy, let's see what you've got."

Like a bullet leaving a pistol, Rufus exploded into action, leaving Amy breathless as he flew over the white sand. She guided him closer to the water's edge and laughed out loud as droplets showered her. Rufus thudded through the surf, his breath coming in snorts. All of Amy's frustration and confusion melted away as she concentrated on Rufus's pounding hooves. Her hair whipped back as she leaned closer to Rufus's neck and urged him to go even faster. This was exactly what she needed — a chance to remember just how incredible it was to feel a connection with a horse, to share their speed and their strength, and earn their trust. Suddenly, she felt ready to devote herself to Impala, no matter what happened with Alfredo.

✥

An hour later, Amy rode Rufus back onto the yard. For once, no one emerged from the stable at the sound of horse hooves, and she was able to lead Rufus into his stall and untack him herself. Then she led him out into the aisle and side-tied him so she could hose him down.

"If I had a white flag, I'd be waving it," Alfredo's voice came from behind her.

Amy spun around. "Me, too. I'm sorry I got so mad before." She was suddenly a little embarrassed about the way she'd reacted.

Alfredo and Amy smiled at each other and then she returned her attention to hosing Rufus's flank. "I was thinking about Impala when I was riding. Do you have to ride her in the match tomorrow?" she asked. "Maybe we should ease the pressure off her until she starts to show signs of improvement in the home arena."

Alfredo sighed. "I need to take my whole string. We'll be playing five chukkers." Amy raised her eyebrows questioningly. "A chukker is a period of play," he explained. "For every chukker, we change horses. I could use some of the others twice but that's putting a lot of pressure on them. And if I don't ride Impala, it would be like admitting I'd been beaten by my horse." His voice was thick with emotion.

Amy was startled. Alfredo couldn't possibly think Impala's behavior was deliberate — that she was trying to *beat* him. It was clear from her earlier reaction that her behavior was rooted in fear.

Alfredo gave her an apologetic smile. "Sorry. I guess this whole thing is really getting to me."

Amy reached out and squeezed his arm. "Don't worry. I understand."

"How about I help you finish up with Rufus and then you can talk me through those flower remedies?"

"Sure." Amy handed Alfredo a sweat scraper and watched him draw it down Rufus's neck. She wished that Papa and the Escobar team members would reassure Alfredo that they had confidence in him. *Right now, whether they mean to or not, they're allowing Alfredo to convince himself that he's bad for the team*, she thought.

After they had put on Rufus's rug and led him into his stall, Amy hurried back to the house to get her case of Bach Flower Remedies, and then joined Alfredo outside Impala's stall.

"I talked with Chrissie. She's going to start turning Impala out in an adjoining paddock so she's on her own but can still see the others," Alfredo said as Amy walked up to the stall. "She's checking the tack for tomorrow's game right now but she asked if later you could talk her through the remedies you want Impala to have."

"Absolutely." Amy nodded. She drew back the bolt on Impala's stall. "Hey, girl."

Impala had been dozing and she looked at them sleepily. "This is a mixture of the remedies I mentioned earlier." Amy held up a bottle. "I'm going to add them to her water." She put a few drops into Impala's automatic drinker. "I've put some into a spritzer, too. Do you want to spray some for her?"

Alfredo took the spritzer from Amy and sprayed it rather self-consciously in the four corners of Impala's stall. He turned to watch the mare, who had been watching him with her ears pricked. Impala gave a sleepy sigh. "She doesn't seem to have noticed the spray," Alfredo remarked disappointedly as Impala moved to her hay net.

"It takes time," Amy reassured him. She unbuckled Impala's red-and-yellow-striped stable rug.

"What are you doing now?" Alfredo asked.

"T-touch with lavender," Amy replied. "Lavender has amazing relaxing properties and T-touch is a form of massage. Put the two together . . ."

"Are we trying to relax her?" Alfredo frowned. "I need her on her toes for tomorrow's game, just not freaking out, that's all."

"It's all about security, trust, and bonding. Those are the things that Impala needs to fulfill her potential. In the wild, horses groom one another to bond, and if Impala's being bullied, then she's missing out on that. We need to start replacing it for her," Amy told him. "T-touch is an even more intense form of grooming. It will give us faster results." She placed her fingers on Impala's neck and began to move them in slow circles. Alfredo watched carefully. She worked her way down to Impala's shoulder, feeling the mare begin to relax under her fingertips. Impala sighed and half closed her eyes. "Now it's your turn. You do the other side," Amy told Alfredo.

"Me?" His eyebrows shot up. "I've never done this before."

"You don't have to get it exactly right for her to appreciate what you're trying to do," she told him.

Alfredo took a step back and looked uncertain.

"Here. Place your hand like this." She lifted Alfredo's hand, which dwarfed her own, and placed it on Impala's neck. "Now move your fingers in small circles." She arched his fingers, and worked them over Impala's coat. The moment Alfredo got a rhythm going, she took her hand away.

Impala shifted her weight and gave a long sigh.

"Good," Amy said. "Now try it with some of this." She unscrewed the top of her lavender bottle. The stall filled with a soothing, heady smell as Alfredo worked a few drops of the liquid into Impala's coat.

"OK," Amy said after a while. "That's probably enough for today."

Alfredo patted Impala's neck. "Good girl. You enjoyed that, didn't you?"

Impala turned her head and nibbled his shirt.

"If Chrissie could turn Impala out on her own so that

our work isn't undone by bullying, then we might see some improvement in her tomorrow," Amy said.

"But not enough to alter her behavior during the game?" Alfredo prompted.

Amy shook her head, and said reluctantly, "Probably not."

❧

Amy set her alarm for quarter to six the next morning so she could do some T-touch on Impala before preparing for the polo game.

Music played across the yard from the open doors of the barn.

"Good morning," Amy called to Joe as he passed her, carrying a bucket and sponge.

"Hey, Amy," he said with a smile.

Another stable hand had Wayward cross-tied in the center of the aisle while his stall was being mucked out. Amy ducked under one of the ties and saw Chrissie in with Palma, bandaging up his tail so it wouldn't get in the way of the play in today's game.

"I'm just going to spend ten minutes with Impala, if that's OK?" Amy called through the stall's bars.

"She's eating," Chrissie said. "But she loves being pampered, so go right ahead."

"Do you need a hand getting her ready?" Amy offered.

"I'm good, thanks," Chrissie told her. "But could you

take her rug off? I'll be in to see to her once I'm finished with Palma."

"Of course," Amy said, and walked to the next stall. "Hello, girl." She slid back the door.

Impala looked up, munching a mouthful of food, and set her ears back slightly.

"Don't worry, I'm not here to take away your break-fast," Amy promised.

As she began massaging Impala, the horse swung her quarters away. Amy moved with her and started again. A wheelbarrow clanked somewhere on the aisle and Impala ran backward. *She's a lot more edgy than yesterday,* Amy observed. Impala obviously knew from all of the activity that it was a match day. Her muscles felt taut under Amy's fingers.

Chrissie came into the stall. "How's she doing?"

"She's pretty tense," Amy admitted. "One day of T-touch and a dose of Bach Flower Remedies can't work miracles."

She wished again that Impala wasn't going to be used today. She stroked Impala's nose. "I'll see you later."

The mare nuzzled her shoulder.

"I'll be rooting for you," Amy murmured.

🙢

The polo grounds were full of activity when they arrived at the field. Amy followed behind the Escobar horse trucks in a chauffeured car with Susannah and Papa. The driver parked alongside the horse trailer. "Let's go wish them luck," Susannah said as she opened the door and climbed out into the sun.

Amy headed toward the back of the trailers. A tall olive-skinned man with graying hair was overseeing the dropping of the ramps. Pablo stood alongside him. "Ah, Ricardo. This is Amy."

Ricardo turned and shook Amy's hand. "It's good to meet you," he said as his warm, strong hand gripped Amy's. "Alfredo's told me a lot about your work. Are you looking forward to the match?"

"Very much," Amy said. "I've never seen a polo match before." She stood back as the first ramp was lowered.

Alfredo appeared around the side of the truck, wearing tall brown boots and a green jersey with TEAM ESCOBAR written on the front.

"Maybe we'll turn you into a fan, eh?" Ricardo said before he walked up the ramp.

"Definitely," Amy said, meeting Alfredo's dark gaze. "Good luck out there," she told him.

Pablo led Wayward down the ramp. The gelding looked around the field as he came out of the trailer, his ears pricked and his eyes shining with excitement.

"Amy." Susannah joined her. "We're going to head over to the members' area. Will you join us?"

Amy would have loved to have stayed to help get the horses ready but she knew that the team had an established routine. "Sure," she agreed.

"Good luck," Susannah said, kissing Pablo's cheek. "We'll see you at halftime."

Papa stayed behind to talk to Ricardo while Amy walked with Susannah over to a large white tent. Susannah was wearing a white pantsuit with a red camisole. Amy glanced down at her own jeans and T-shirt and suddenly felt underdressed.

Susannah slipped her arm through Amy's. "One of the things I love about polo is that there are no hard-and-fast rules for the spectator. There's no dress code, you get to watch the game from a deck chair, and no one cares if you sip soda or champagne!"

Amy felt a rush of gratitude for Susannah's sensitivity. "I *was* wondering if I was underdressed," she admitted.

"You're fine," Susannah reassured her.

Near the entrance to the tent, photographers stood on either side snapping shots of the members as they walked into it.

"Just keep going," Susannah murmured as a flashlight went off in Amy's face.

They hurried into the tent, and Amy felt immediate relief from the coolness offered by the shade.

"Susannah!" A tall red-haired woman wearing a feathered hat hurried over to them. She kissed Susannah on each cheek before turning to Amy. Her spicy perfume filled the air. "I'm Jasmine. My husband is the manager of Silver Birch."

"Silver Birch is the team we're playing today," Susannah explained.

"Nice to meet you," Amy said.

"Amy's staying with us at the moment. She's a friend of Alfredo's," Susannah told the woman.

"Well, enjoy the game, Amy," Jasmine said. But then her face got serious. "Although," she turned back to Susannah, "I'm afraid I can't wish your team the *very* best!"

"Don't worry, we won't be cheering your team on from the sidelines, either," Susannah responded with a playful smile. "But we hope they come in a respectable second."

Susannah introduced Amy to various other people. "I hope you don't mind if I don't say why you're staying with us," she said in a low voice as they went to get a drink from the tables at the back of the tent. "Alfredo's mortified enough about his problems with Impala without me drawing more attention to them."

"I had a feeling," Amy admitted. She thought how lucky Alfredo was to have such an understanding stepparent.

"Come on," Susannah said. "They'll be starting soon." She handed Amy a glass of fresh lemonade and led her outside to a row of navy-and-white-striped deck chairs set up underneath gazebos.

Amy blinked at the size of the polo pitch. It was much bigger than she had expected, about ten times the size of a soccer field. She sat down in her chair as the polo teams cantered out and took their positions. The players were wearing face protectors, and if it hadn't been for Archie, she would never have known which rider was Alfredo. The gelding was on the bit and prancing. Like all the other horses, he was decked out in double reins, a breast-plate, and a standing martingale. His legs were protected by bandages and bell boots.

Amy felt a thrill of excitement as the two teams lined up to face each other. One of the mounted umpires threw in the ball and the first chukker began. In a thunder of hooves, the riders were off. The horses were so closely bunched that it seemed as if several of them might collide at any moment.

Susannah passed Amy something. "You can use these to follow the play." Amy looked down and saw a tiny pair of binoculars. She adjusted them for her eyes and tried looking through them at the field. Now she was able to see the ball and the players' interactions much more clearly. She looked up to inspect the scoreboard and was surprised to see that the other team had already been awarded points, despite the fact that nothing had happened in the game yet.

"Why does Silver Birch already have a score on the board?" Amy asked.

"It's to make the teams as equal as possible," Susannah replied. "Teams are given handicaps, and if there's any difference between two teams, the weaker team is given a head start in the score."

Amy lifted her binoculars to watch the play as it headed down the field. Alfredo was up front. He swung his mallet in a downward circle to give the ball a tremendous hit toward the goal. As he galloped after it, Amy saw one of the opposition in his bright red team shirt cut in front of Archie, forcing him to swerve.

"Foul!" Susannah cried just as the umpire stopped play. She leaned into Amy and explained, "Crossing the line of the ball isn't allowed."

Amy nodded. She could see how that could be a dangerous maneuver.

Alfredo was awarded a free shot from midfield. Amy peered through the binoculars as he swung back his mallet. *Come on, Alfredo!* she cheered silently. She was amazed at how still Archie stood as the mallet swung down beside him and cracked against the ball. Amy followed the ball's flight through the air and between the two goalposts.

"Yes!" She jumped to her feet and began to clap. "Go, Alfredo!"

The couple sitting on the other side of Amy called over. "Looks like there will be another cup for the Escobar cabinet, eh, Susannah?"

"Beware the commentator's curse," Susannah said, laughing. "The moment you predict a win is the moment it all falls apart."

Amy sat back down. "Why is Alfredo chasing the ball at the Escobar goal now?" she asked as she watched Alfredo reverse the direction of his play.

"Every time a goal is scored, they swap ends," Susannah told her. "There are a lot of rules to the game — it took me ages to understand it all!"

Amy took a sharp breath as the Silver Birch's number two blocked a swing by Alfredo with his mallet and stole the ball. The players reined the horses around to pursue the ball in the opposite direction.

"Can he do that?" Amy asked.

"He sure can," Susannah replied.

The thirty second bell clanged to warn that the end of the first chukker was coming up.

Pablo, who was the team's number three, was in fast pursuit of the ball. He galloped Lily at breakneck speed to reach the opposing team's number one player. Lily's stride shortened as she drew behind the chestnut, and Pablo leaned forward to hook the number one's mallet just as the player was about to hit the ball. Amy lost sight of the ball as Pablo swung his mallet back. She searched the field and saw that Pablo had shot the ball a huge distance back up the field.

"That's Jaime," Susannah murmured as the Escobar

rider in the number four shirt collected the ball and hit it to Alfredo.

Amy's fingers tightened against her binoculars as Alfredo took a shot at the goal. The ball scudded to the side, just missing the post. Amy's heart sank. It would have been an amazing start to Alfredo's game if he had scored two goals in the first chukker. A horn blared to end the chukker, and Amy joined the crowd's applause as the teams changed their horses.

To her surprise, when Alfredo reappeared, he was riding Impala. "Why is he riding her so soon?" she whispered to Susannah.

"Maybe he just wants to get it over and done with," Susannah said in a low voice. Her brown eyes looked worried as she followed Alfredo and Impala.

"She doesn't look happy," Amy murmured. The mare was hunched up beneath the saddle and, unlike the other horses whose bandaged tails were carried high, Impala's was clamped firmly down.

The teams galloped after the ball as it headed toward the Escobar goal. When Alfredo tried to send her after the play, she refused to open up her stride. The rest of the team took off after the ball and Alfredo was left behind as Impala skittered sideways.

"Come on, Impala," Susannah urged.

The mare finally straightened and her stride lengthened into a gallop. As the play went farther away, Amy raised her binoculars. Alfredo was gaining on the Silver Birch number one player, who had possession of the ball. Alfredo leaned across to hook the player's mallet, but Impala swerved away. Alfredo fell forward onto the mare's neck and Amy gripped Susannah's arm as he struggled to get back into the saddle. He was caught up in the middle of the teams' horses on all sides of him, when Impala reared. Alfredo dropped his weight forward to bring Impala back down.

"She's never done that before!" Susannah gasped. "She seems to be getting worse with every match."

The Silver Birch number one swung at the ball, which flew between the posts. A groan went up from the Escobar supporters.

For the rest of the chukker, Alfredo fought Impala. Although the mare would chase after the action, the moment Alfredo tried to get anywhere near the tussle for the ball, Impala would shy away.

She looks so scared, Amy thought. The whites of Impala's eyes were showing as Alfredo raised his mallet to pass the ball to Pablo. He missed his shot as Impala plunged forward. The thirty second warning bell rang as Silver Birch gained possession of the ball and galloped down the field.

Amy felt her mouth go dry as their number one player took a shot at the goal. *Please don't score, please don't score,* she pleaded to herself. But the ball rolled through the posts, giving Silver Birch the lead.

The horn sounded and Susannah reached out to squeeze Amy's hand.

Alfredo rode off the field, his shoulders slumped. Now that she was leaving the field, Impala was trotting obediently, but her flanks and neck were wet with sweat.

Amy's heart sank. After that performance, Alfredo would be convinced that his place on the team was more vulnerable than ever.

Chapter Eight

❧

As Amy changed into a long cream-colored skirt and wraparound top, her thoughts were not so much on her outfit as on the meal ahead. Juan, Jaime, and Ricardo were joining the family for dinner and a discussion of the match.

Amy hadn't seen Alfredo since he'd left the field. He hadn't joined her and Susannah to stamp the divots on the pitch at halftime, and as soon as he got home, he had retreated to his room.

Amy stopped at the mirror to give her hair one last check before heading down. She wished she knew what to say to Alfredo over dinner. She had an uneasy feeling that he might be wondering just why he had invited her to stay. Everything that Amy had seen of Impala's behavior on the pitch pointed toward her being bullied. The moment she had come into contact with the other horses, she had fought to get away. *She was genuinely scared today,* Amy thought, remembering Impala's reactions to the match. But she still couldn't fully commit to that theory. Impala had been so happy and relaxed when she had ridden out with Archie; if she were really unhappy in equine company, would she have been so calm then?

"But if it's not bullying, what else could it be?" she asked her reflection as she pushed the back onto a gold earring. Impala had perfect breeding, a perfect upbringing, a perfect home, and perfect training. *She is the perfect pony.* Amy sighed. None of this made sense.

She walked down to the living room where the family was having a predinner drink. Amy poured herself some juice at the buffet and looked around the room for Alfredo. He wasn't there.

"Amy." Pablo waved her over. "Come meet the rest of the family."

She walked over to the fireplace, where Pablo was chatting with Juan and Jaime. "Amy, this is my brother, Juan, and my nephew, Jaime." Pablo introduced her to two broad-shouldered men who both had the Escobar dark brown eyes and raven hair.

"I really enjoyed watching you play today," Amy said as Juan, then Jaime, kissed her cheek.

"Thank you, although it's a shame you didn't come to a match we won," Jaime said.

"I guess you can't win them all," Amy replied. "But it was the first match I've been to, and I thought the whole thing was amazing. The way the horses respond is incredible."

"Years and years of your coach yelling at you will teach you to forge that kind of connection with a horse, trust me." Jaime winked.

"I abused you? And here I thought I was being too easy on you," Ricardo said as he joined them. "What did you think of the game today, Amy?"

"There was a lot to follow," Amy admitted. "But I loved watching the play."

Ellen, the housekeeper, walked into the room. "Dinner is ready," she announced.

Amy followed Ricardo into the dining room. A huge oval table was set with china, crystal glasses, and silver cutlery. Hundreds of little lights danced across the surface of the table, reflected from the chandelier above. She sat alongside Ricardo and noted that Alfredo still hadn't made an appearance. She glanced at Susannah, wondering if she would be upset that he hadn't turned up for dinner.

Susannah met Amy's gaze and smiled. She raised her glass and called for the attention of the group. "I'd just like to thank Amy for sacrificing time out of her busy schedule to be with us."

"To Amy," everyone echoed, raising their glasses.

The door opened and Alfredo walked in. "Sorry I'm late," he apologized quietly to Susannah as he pulled out his seat.

"That's OK." Susannah smiled. "It's allowed. You had a tough day."

"Another one," Papa grunted. "We never seem to get good days anymore."

Amy tensed and looked at Alfredo. His cheeks were flushed and he was staring down at his place setting.

Two servers walked in, one carrying a large tureen on a silver tray. They made their way around the table and ladled something into each person's bowl. Amy picked up her spoon once she had been served and looked down at her chilled soup. She suddenly didn't feel very hungry. What she really wanted was to talk with Alfredo about what had happened today. She watched him push his spoon from one side of the bowl to the other.

Alfredo looked up and met her eyes. "So, I guess you got to see what Impala's really like today, huh?" His voice was low.

Amy hesitated. *Was* today the real Impala? Somehow she didn't think so. She couldn't reconcile the frightened, disobedient horse she'd observed today with the sweet-natured mare she had gotten to know since her arrival.

"So, what is your diagnosis now that you have seen our mare in action?" Papa's voice cut though the murmur of conversation. "Do you still think putting her in a paddock on her own will cure her?"

Amy's cheeks grew hot as she realized everyone's attention had turned to her. "There's a lot about Impala that doesn't add up," she said carefully. "She hasn't suffered any trauma, she loves to please, her diet is fine, and she's not in any physical pain. I know that she's followed the same training program as all the Escobar horses, so she shouldn't have any fear of the mallet or ball, and Alfredo's an experienced rider. So the only thing left for me to work with at the moment is that she has a fear of being overcrowded by other horses."

"But will separating her from the others in the home paddock make that fear disappear?" Ricardo asked as he broke a piece of bread.

Amy shook her head. "Not on its own. Horses have long memories, so while it will make Impala happier on a day-to-day basis, it won't cure her panic at being in a group of horses. Hopefully, the Bach Flower Remedies will begin to help her deal with her fears. Over time she could be gradually reintroduced to other horses."

"So you're saying that if she is being bullied, it's going to take a long time before she's happy being crowded in by other horses. Am I right?" Pablo asked.

Amy hesitated before nodding.

"Which would mean losing her from the team," Juan said heavily. "And we still need to find a replacement for Elvira. We've got nothing but problems at the moment."

Alfredo pushed back his chair. "Maybe you should just say what you mean. You want me off the team."

"Sit down, boy." Papa waved his hand. "You're an Escobar, your place is on that field."

"Some Escobar. I can't even control my horse," Alfredo said bitterly.

"Alfredo, no one doubts that you're a good rider," Susannah said gently.

"No? Well, *I* do!" Alfredo snapped. He looked down the table to his grandfather. "Do *you* think that Impala could be controlled by a rider with more experience?"

Amy stared at Papa, willing him to give Alfredo the reassurance he needed.

"I think perhaps Pablo should put Impala in Elvira's place. We can find a new polo horse for you," the old man replied.

Alfredo's face drained of color. "Is that what everyone thinks?"

"Impala is *your* horse," Pablo said firmly. "The decision is yours."

Alfredo shook his head. "That wasn't what I asked." He looked at Susannah. "You'll have to excuse me, but I've lost my appetite." He dropped his napkin on the table and stalked out of the room.

Amy pushed back her chair. "I think I should see if he's all right," she said.

"Yes. Go," Papa agreed. "Try and talk some sense into the boy."

Amy hurried after Alfredo. She caught up with him as he was letting himself into his room. "Can we talk?"

Alfredo hesitated, and Amy thought for one moment he was going to say that he wanted to be alone. "OK," he said, holding the door open for her.

Alfredo's room was totally different from the rest of the house. A small hallway from the door ended with two steps down into a living room. The waxed pine floor was half covered with a black-and-white-checkered rug. Opposite the entrance, French doors stood open to a large balcony facing the backyard. Black leather sofas faced one wall of the room where a flat-screen television hung over a fireplace. On the other side of the room was a small kitchen area.

Alfredo walked into the living room and sat down in a leather armchair. Amy sat near him on one of the sofas. "I'm really sorry about today," she said softly.

Alfredo tried to smile. "Which part?"

"No one doubts that you're an amazing rider," Amy told him. "You were terrific today, and no one could have handled Impala better. I'm sure she would have bolted no matter who was riding her. Whenever a horse gets scared, its impulse is to run. The fact that you kept Impala in the game just shows what a great job you were doing."

Alfredo sighed and ran his fingers over his hair. "Thanks, Amy. That means a lot. I wish other people had that much confidence in me."

"Everyone just wants what's best for you and the team," Amy said. "Listen, tomorrow morning, I'd like to join up with Impala."

Alfredo's eyebrows crinkled together. "Join up?"

"It's a way of developing, or deepening, trust," Amy told him. "Impala's showing fear out on the polo field, and one of the ways we can help her overcome that is by building up her trust."

Alfredo leaned forward. "This has worked for you with other horses?"

Amy hesitated. She'd seen joining-up work wonders, but she didn't want to give Alfredo false hope. Everything about Impala's personality was contradictory to her behavior on the field. Amy couldn't be sure that a join-up would help. "It all depends on how deeply rooted her issues are, but it is a very effective method," she admitted. "The first time I ever did a join-up, my mother talked me through it. My pony, Sundance, was having trust issues with me and the join-up really turned us around." She took a deep breath. "I've got so much to thank my mom for." She was hoping this might lead Alfredo to bring up his own mother, but he didn't.

"I know that if anyone can make a breakthrough, it's you."

Amy felt her stomach twist. The truth was, the mare might never be happy being crowded in by a group of horses. But looking at the hope in Alfredo's eyes, she knew she couldn't tell him that. "I'll try my best," she said. "I promise."

Alfredo leaned closer, his eyes locked on hers. Amy's heart to began to race. She knew that if she didn't break the spell between them, Alfredo would kiss her. *Would that be so bad?* a voice argued in her head as she felt herself melting under the gaze of his deep brown eyes. Reluctantly, Amy pulled back and looked away. Getting involved with Alfredo now would distract her from her work with Impala. *And if I really care about Alfredo, then I won't do anything to jeopardize a breakthrough with Impala,* Amy tried to convince herself. But she could tell that this voice of reason was not one she wanted to hear.

❧

Amy got to the stable early the next morning to spend some time with Impala. Once she had massaged lavender oil into the mare's coat, she moved up to her head.

"What was yesterday all about, huh?" she asked the mare, who nuzzled her shoulder. Amy studied Impala's wide, honest-looking eyes. "I wish you could tell me what's making you so scared."

"Morning." Alfredo slid back the door and walked into the stall. He held out his hand to Impala, who stretched out her neck to sniff him. She blew in disappointment.

"No cookies?" Amy asked.

"Sorry, girl," Alfredo said, patting Impala's hip. "But snacking isn't good for your waistline."

"Believe me," Amy said as she clipped on Impala's lead line, "she'll run off the calories in no time."

"I'm looking forward to seeing how this works," Alfredo told her as they walked down to the outside arena. He opened the arena gate and closed it behind them. "It's great to think we're going to make some progress with Impala." He stroked the mare's neck and looked at her affectionately.

Amy felt worried that Alfredo was expecting too much from a single join-up. "It all takes time," she reminded him.

Alfredo nodded and climbed up onto the gate to watch.

Amy led Impala into the center of the arena. She halted the mare and unclipped the lead rein. Impala stood quietly, and when Amy shooed her away she looked uncertain. Her nostrils flared when Amy flicked the lead rope, and she shied over to the fence. *She is such a sensitive pony,* Amy thought as Impala trotted around the ring.

She flicked the lead line again and Impala's canter became a gallop. The mare's stride ate up the ground as she traveled around and around the arena. Impala's inside ear and eye were riveted on Amy. Confusion showed in her eyes. Amy, who had become her friend, was now driving her away.

Just as Amy felt a fresh surge of determination that she could figure this horse out, she noticed Impala's stride slacken. The mare lowered her head and gave Amy the sign that she wanted to stop running. She worked her jaw as if she were chewing gum. All of her body language told Amy that she wanted to be friends. She took a step ahead of Impala's action and the mare slowed. She took a step back and Impala's pace quickened.

Finally, Amy turned her back on Impala. It didn't make any difference that the sound she was waiting for was one that she had heard so many times before. When the soft thud of Impala's hooves on the sand reached her, she felt a rush of joy. She stepped forward and stopped, and then stepped to the side and stopped, as if she were following the steps of a favorite dance. Wherever she went, Impala traced her footsteps. After several minutes, Amy turned around and slid her arms around the mare's neck. Impala sighed and rested her head on Amy's shoulder.

"I think you want to tell me what's wrong just as much as I want you to," Amy whispered, stroking the horse's mane.

As she turned to walk back to the gate, Amy saw that Pablo had joined Alfredo.

"I thought you didn't have a magic wand." Alfredo grinned as Amy approached.

"I don't," she protested, clipping on Impala's lead line.

"So how is it done?" Pablo asked, looking impressed.

Amy smiled and she reached up to stroke the mare's cheek. "Horses naturally belong in a herd, and in that herd is an alpha horse — the leader that all the others trust to lead them to food and protect them from danger. By chasing Impala away, I take the role of the alpha horse and get her to accept the fact that what she really wants is to be *with* me, not against me."

Pablo nodded. "It makes sense."

"She sees me as the alpha horse because I dominated her. She's decided to put her trust in me, and the sign of that is the way she follows me wherever I go," Amy finished.

"Now if we could just attach the ball to you in the next polo match, Impala and I will be fine," Alfredo joked. He jumped off the gate to rub Impala's nose.

Pablo looked thoughtful. "Both of you wait here. I'll be back in a few minutes."

Amy watched Alfredo's father as he walked quickly

toward the stables. "Where do you think he's going?" Amy asked Alfredo, who shrugged in response.

When Pablo returned, he was carrying Impala's tack along with a mallet bag. "Tack her up," he said, placing the saddle, bridle, and martingale on the gate.

Amy thought it was a good idea to get Alfredo into the saddle right after the join-up.

Alfredo helped her to tack up Impala, but Amy was taken aback when Pablo handed her the hat. "Alfredo should ride," she argued.

"But you just did the join-up. I would like to see what she does for you," Pablo said firmly.

Amy glanced at Alfredo and was relieved to see that he looked relaxed about the suggestion. "Here," he said as she fumbled with her chin strap. "Let me help."

Alfredo adjusted the strap and then boosted Amy up into the saddle. "Good luck," he said as he handed her the mallet.

This time the mallet didn't feel quite as unnatural as before. Holding the reins in one hand, Amy urged Impala into the center of the arena. She reined the mare around and got her to canter as Pablo tossed the ball toward them. As the ball scudded past, she reined Impala around again and gave chase. She brought the mallet back as they bore down on the ball and then swung it forward again like a giant pendulum. With a loud *crack* the ball flew into the air. Impala shot after it, and Amy let out a whoop of delight. She rode past the ball before reining Impala around and aiming at it once again. This time when she hit it, the ball scudded almost down to the gate. Amy let Impala out fully but had only seconds to slow her as they ran out of ground.

Alfredo and Pablo were both clapping. Amy halted Impala and leaned forward to pat her neck. "That was terrific! You were great!"

"You both did well. Are you sure you've never played before?" Pablo asked, smiling broadly.

"Maybe she *should* play," Alfredo said. "There's the mixed scrimmage coming up at our local club at the end of next week. Amy could play in that."

"I wouldn't be good enough," Amy protested, dropping her stirrups and slipping off Impala's back. "Don't forget, I wasn't riding with any other horses just now."

"I'll train you," Alfredo said, his dark eyes sparkling. "It's the least I can do to thank you for all the work you're putting in on Impala. You can't leave without having the full polo experience."

Amy's mouth went dry. "I couldn't. One of the horses might end up getting hurt. And I can't guarantee that Impala's going to be ready to play with other horses."

Pablo slapped Alfredo on the back. "I'll leave you to convince our guest." He took Impala's reins. "Come on, girl. Let's get you to your stall."

Amy's heart thudded as she faced Alfredo. "I really don't think it's a good idea."

Alfredo reached out and held both of her hands. "I trust you to do what's best for Impala. Will you trust me in return to get you ready for the game?"

Amy knew she had more than enough on her plate just working with Impala. Now he wanted her to learn a totally new sport? The idea of riding in a match *was* exhilarating. . . . She paused and allowed the idea of training with Alfredo to sink in. She pictured his string of horses, and how she would get to ride each one of them. *And I would still get to work with Impala and maybe even get her ready for a match,* she thought. Excitement won out, and, even though she knew it was crazy, she nodded.

"OK." She smiled. "I trust you."

Chapter Nine

❧

Alfredo and Pablo wanted to check on Elvira after the training session, so Amy walked back to the house alone. As she walked up the driveway, a limousine drew up alongside her and the driver's window rolled down. "Señor Escobar Senior would like the pleasure of your company if you are not otherwise occupied," the chauffeur said.

Amy was too startled to reply as the driver stopped the car and got out. He opened the rear door and Amy saw Papa sitting inside. She felt her mouth slacken and wasn't sure what to do.

"Are you going to keep me waiting all day, girl?" Papa asked. His tone was stern but there was something playful about the look in his eyes.

Curiosity got the better of Amy, and she slid onto the seat opposite Papa. He was dressed in crisp, casual clothes and a Panama hat. "Where are we going?"

She thought for a moment that Papa wasn't going to answer her. He stared out the window as they drove down the driveway. "To a neighboring stud farm," he said eventually. "It's just a ten-minute drive away."

Amy realized that he wasn't going to volunteer any more information. She looked out her own window as they left the Escobar estate behind and drove out into open country. Why did Papa want her company? He'd always made it perfectly clear that he had little time for her, and no faith in the methods she used.

A wooden sign at the side of the road announced in swirly writing that they had reached Cedar View Stud Farm. The car turned and drove past fields full of horses: sleek Arabians, Thoroughbreds, and quarter horses. Spider-legged foals chased one another in the sun while their mothers dozed under the shade of huge leafy trees. The road dipped down and the stud farm was visible ahead. The long, low building looked more like a ranch than the Escobars' luxurious estate. The car drove around the back of the house and parked near two large barns. When the chauffeur opened the door, Papa swept his hand to indicate Amy should get out first.

A tall, slim woman, her blond hair pulled back in a

ponytail, walked out of the first of the barns. "Señor Escobar!" She waved, her face lighting up.

Papa slowly climbed out of the car. "Jess," he acknowledged, and walked to meet her.

Amy hovered uncertainly, not knowing if she should go with Papa or wait where she was.

"Come," Papa called over his shoulder. "I want to introduce you to a good friend of mine."

Amy walked down to the woman, who was just kissing Papa on each cheek. She then turned to shake Amy's hand. "I'm Jessica Hammond. It's good to meet you," she said warmly. She turned back to Papa. "Thanks so much for coming."

"It's a pleasure, my dear, even if you are trying to set up competition for me." Papa's dark eyes twinkled.

"Oh, I'll never be a threat to the famous Escobar bloodline," Jess said as she took his arm. She must have noticed the look of confusion on Amy's face because she explained, "I want to start breeding polo ponies. I bought a rather special purebred Criollo horse last week and I asked Señor Escobar out here to look at her."

They walked into the barn and passed a stable hand who was hosing down the walkway. The stalls were all empty, with the exception of the first one. A dun mare with a long black mane watched them approach. "I'm keeping Amber Nectar in isolation until she completes her deworming program and gets all her shots," Jess explained. She pulled back the door and stepped into the box with its deep bed of straw.

"She looks as if she's settling in well," Papa said as he ran his eyes over Amber Nectar. The mare stretched out to sniff his hand. "She's not showing any signs of stress and her flanks are filled out."

Jess nodded. "Amber's got the best appetite on the yard!"

"What do you think, Amy?" Papa's question took her by surprise.

She studied the horse for a moment before responding. "I don't know what the Criollo standard is, so I can't say if she's a good example of the breed," Amy began apologetically.

Papa waved his hand in a dismissive gesture. "Tell me what you can see, not what you can't."

Amy looked into the mare's alert eyes, set in a wide forehead below small pointed ears. She let her hand trail down Amber's warm neck, noting the long, heavy shoulder. She continued on down Amber's leg, which was surprisingly short but solid, with strong joints. Amy then stood back and took in the mare's short, straight back and well-muscled hindquarters. She wasn't a conventionally beautiful horse, lacking the delicate lines of an Arabian or the noble head of a Thoroughbred, but she was symmetrical and well-shaped, with strength in every muscle. "Her eyes and ears tell me she's intelligent, a real thinker. Her body is pure brawn, though. She looks as if she was bred for endurance above finesse. I'd certainly want to be on her if I had to fight my way out of a difficult situation."

Papa grunted. "Criollo horses are the direct descendants of the warhorses of the New World. They were imported by Spanish conquistadores five hundred years ago. Over the centuries they adapted to living in the South American plains. They developed endurance, hardiness, and a fearless, independent nature." He ran his hand over Amber just as Amy had done. "She's a good example," he told Jess. "But I'd like to see her under the saddle before I give you my final opinion."

Jess nodded and leaned over the door. "Can you bring me Amber's tack, Zach?" she called. She smiled at Amy. "Señor Escobar tells me you're staying with the family for a while."

Amy nodded. "Alfredo asked me to come out to help him work with one of his horses."

"You work with horses, too?" Amy nodded in response and Jess seemed to consider this before going on.

"I'm sorry, I didn't get your last name," Jess said.

"Fleming," Amy told her.

Jess's eyes widened. "As in Marion Fleming? The British show jumper?"

"And more lately the owner of Heartland." Amy nodded, feeling the familiar rush of pride for her mother.

"I've read all about your work," Jess said enthusiastically, her green eyes bright with interest. "In fact, I use many of your methods here."

Behind Amy, Papa had a sudden coughing fit.

"Are you OK?" Jess hurried forward, sounding alarmed. "Would you like some water?"

Papa shook his head. "I'll be all right. It's probably the dust in the air, that's all."

"Well, the sooner we get outdoors, the better," Jess said as the stable hand brought in Amber's tack. "Thanks, Zach."

Amy gave Jess a hand to saddle Amber in the full western saddle. She fastened the throatlatch and then gently pulled the mare's long forelock from under the brow band. She rubbed Amber's rounded nose. "You're all set," she told her.

Jess took Amber's reins and led her out of her stall. Amy and Papa followed as the mare walked calmly out of the entrance and over to the schooling arena alongside the barn.

Jess turned to Amy. "I'd love to see you ride her. Would you like to?"

Amy was touched by Jess's confidence in her. "Sure." She felt a buzz of excitement at the prospect of riding an unfamiliar purebred. She took Amber's reins and led her over to the mounting block close to the fence. Amber stood still while she settled into the deep, comfortable western saddle.

Jess held open the gate for Amy to ride into the arena. Once they were inside, Amy trotted in a figure eight and then halted. She squeezed with her legs without releasing the pressure on her reins, and Amber took three quick steps back. "Good girl." Amy leaned forward and patted her neck. The mare snorted and tossed her head, making her mane bounce against her neck and shoulder.

Amy trotted her around the arena once more before sending her into a canter. The mare's short stride was surprisingly smooth as she covered the distance from one end of the arena to the other. When they reached the next long side, Amy gave the mare her head. Amber's agility as she took each corner at a full gallop reminded Amy of Alfredo's polo ponies and how they could turn on a dime.

"OK, bring her in now," Papa finally called opening the gate.

Amy trotted Amber over and halted alongside Papa and Jess. She dropped her stirrups and slid off. "Good girl," she said, patting Amber's neck. "I enjoyed that."

Papa examined the inside of the mare's mouth and listened to her breathing.

"What did you think of her?" Jess asked Amy.

"I was expecting a less comfortable ride than she gave me because of her short legs. But her paces are surprisingly smooth. Her mouth's soft and she was really easy to handle; she did everything I asked her to do right away," Amy replied.

Jess rested her hand on Amber's neck. "Why do I feel as though you want to add 'but' to the end of your sentence?"

Amy smiled. "I guess it's because I felt she was holding back on me. It was as if she was totally happy to have me on her back but there wasn't any interaction between the two of us."

Papa grunted. "It's a trait of the breed. They're often a one-person horse. They don't trust easily, but when they do, they trust completely."

"Then, if you were to encourage her trust through a join-up, I'd imagine she'd be incredible," Amy said to Jess.

"I read all about how you do a join-up although I've never tried it myself," Jess said. "It must be amazing to have a horse choose to work for you instead of using force to get it to bend to your will."

Amy grinned. "It can be the best feeling in the world."

"Not you, too," Papa said, straightening up. "I thought you were a sensible woman, Jess."

Jess's eyebrows shot up. "Do I detect some skepticism here?"

"Papa's still not sold on Heartland's methods," Amy murmured.

"Well, I'm sure if anyone can persuade him that alternative methods are worthwhile, it's you," Jess replied. She stepped forward to take Amber's reins. "So, what do you think of Amber, Señor Escobar?"

"I'd say you've got a good one there," Papa told her. "She's an excellent example of the breed. She's got a willing nature, her limbs are clean, her form is good, and her movement is lovely. But you won't get competitive polo ponies from her if you mate her with another pure-bred Criollo."

Jess nodded as they began to walk back to the barn. "I was thinking of breeding her with Desert Star, my Arabian stallion."

Zach came out of the barn and took Amber's reins. "Come on, girl."

"Star's in the other barn. Come see him," Jess offered. She led the way to the next barn.

The stallion stood squarely with his proud neck arched and his large intelligent eyes as round as dark moons. His black coat gleamed, and Amy reached forward to run her hand down his satiny neck. Desert Star swung his head to look at her, and Amy caught her breath when she saw the full beauty of his dished face. "You're a gorgeous boy, aren't you?" she said softly.

"You'd get an excellent combination of strength, agility, and speed from the two horses," Papa said. "You might even persuade me to buy one of their foals!"

Jess laughed. "You'll get first choice, I promise."

The three of them began to walk back toward the waiting limousine. "Well, it was lovely meeting you, Amy," Jess said warmly. "Feel free to drop by again before you leave."

"Thanks," Amy said. "It was nice meeting you, too."

As she walked with Papa back to the car, she wondered why he had invited her along. She had really enjoyed the visit, but she couldn't figure out what Papa had gotten from her company.

Their chauffeur was leaning on the car, reading a newspaper. As they approached, he folded it and tossed it into the car before holding open the rear door.

Amy slid into the cool interior, expecting another silent ride home, but as soon as Papa was seated he said, "I've heard of your mother, Marion Fleming. Why didn't you follow her into show jumping? You ride well."

Amy blinked in surprise at Papa's compliment. "I have ridden competitively, but I want a career with more substance." The moment the words were out of her mouth, she realized that she'd probably insulted Papa. His entire career had been built on competitive riding.

"Ha!" Papa snorted. "You think that this alternative

work you do has substance and yet you have done nothing to improve Impala since you arrived."

"It takes time," Amy replied.

"I'll tell you what has substance." Papa leaned forward and planted his walking stick on the floor of the car. "Substance is in a horse that has hundreds of years of breeding from natural selection so only the fittest and strongest survive. Impala is bred out of the best Criollo and Thoroughbred bloodlines in the world. It took years of selection and breeding to produce her and our other horses. *That* is substance!"

Now it became clear to Amy why Papa had invited her along. He'd wanted to show her that her modern methods had no place with the Escobar horses, whose history was centuries old. But he didn't realize that her approach to horses hadn't been invented this century, nor even the one before that, but went back much, much further.

"Alternative remedies are timeless," Amy responded. "They're based on everything that is natural and reject anything that is artificial. A join-up is horse centered, not person centered. It appeals to the horse's natural instincts and nothing else."

Papa stared at her and it was impossible to gauge his thoughts. "Your mother taught you all this?"

"My mom died several years ago," Amy said quietly. "But yes, I learned from her. It's difficult not having her around to advise me when difficult cases come along and I begin to doubt my own abilities." She took a deep breath. "Where is Alfredo's mom?"

Papa stiffened. "What?"

"Alfredo's going through a tough time. He blames himself for Impala's behavior since he was the one who trained her. I'm sure having his mother around to reassure him would mean the world — which is not to say that Susannah isn't wonderful," she added hastily. "It's just not the same."

Papa's eyes narrowed at Amy. "Alfredo's mother knew nothing of horses," he said. He tipped his hat over his eyes. "Enough conversation. I am tired now."

Amy stared out the window with a feeling of frustration. It was impossible to tell if anything she'd said to Papa had altered his opinion, and she doubted it did.

Chapter Ten

❧

That afternoon, Amy went out onto her balcony and settled into one of the chairs. The sun's rays bathed her as she closed her eyes and pictured the way Alfredo had gazed at her earlier.

Up until now, Alfredo had been so wrapped up in his problems with Impala that he had sometimes seemed distant. Now that he was feeling more optimistic about the horse, he was beginning to show a different side. The more progress they made with Impala, the more tempting it was to keep getting closer to Alfredo. Amy found that when she wasn't busy with other things, her thoughts quickly found their way to her new friend.

She picked up a book she'd borrowed from Pablo on polo technique, but she couldn't concentrate. Her thoughts kept straying to Alfredo. She tried to remember if he'd mentioned a girlfriend but she was sure he hadn't. He was good-looking, successful, charming, and his dedication to Impala was incredibly endearing. Amy gave up on the book. She'd e-mail Soraya instead. Some advice from her best friend about a possible summer romance was exactly what she needed.

Back in her room, Amy flipped open her laptop. She logged on to her e-mail account and noticed an e-mail waiting from Ty. Amy opened it and read the weekly rundown that Ty had gotten into the habit of sending her. She loved keeping up with what was happening at Heartland. Home felt a million miles away right then. She suddenly realized how much she would love to have his perspective on Impala.

She hit the REPLY tab on Ty's e-mail and quickly typed an explanation of Impala's situation. It felt good just putting the whole thing in writing and she looked forward to getting his reply as she hit SEND.

Then she opened up the e-mail that was waiting for her from Soraya.

Hey, Amy.

OK, so what aren't you telling me?! I've never had to do so much reading between the lines! What's Alfredo like, other than a hundred percent focused on his horse? I'm sure you can find a way to get some of that focus onto you. What does he look like? With a name like Alfredo, I'm picturing him as tall, dark, and handsome. If he is, then he sounds like the perfect addition to the amazing summer you're having in the Hamptons.

Amy giggled. She finished reading Soraya's description of her own vacation and hit REPLY.

I should have known that you would cut to the chase about Alfredo! OK, I give in, he is everything you could imagine. The truth is that a summer romance is totally appealing, but should I really get involved when I've only got a couple more weeks before I have to be back at school?
   Anyway, it's great to hear how much fun you're having — hugs to you and Anthony.
   XOXO
   Amy

The next morning, Amy arranged to meet Alfredo for a training session in the arena. She had visited Impala before walking down to the arena, and the mare seemed totally relaxed as she pulled at her hay net.

"Ready?" Alfredo was holding Archie, fully tacked up, inside the gate.

"I still think this whole thing is crazy," Amy told him. "We only have four days!"

"I wouldn't imagine the average person could be ready for a polo match in four days," Alfredo said as he boosted

Amy up into Archie's saddle. "But you're already an experienced rider. I'm going to be teaching you some basic stick-and-ball moves. Don't forget that it's just a friendly match you'll be playing in."

"I hope the emphasis is on 'friendly,'" Amy said.

Alfredo tipped back his head and laughed. "I won't let anyone hurt you," he promised. "How about I run through some rules while you warm Archie up?"

Amy checked her girth and nodded. She clicked to Archie and settled into his stride as they rode a large circle around Alfredo.

"The most important thing for you to remember is the line of the ball. Whoever has the line of the ball on their right has the right of way. The only way this changes is if the player is moved away from the line of the ball."

Amy remembered the shoulder-to-shoulder contact at the match between the players.

"You're allowed to push an opponent off the line, hook his mallet, bump his horse, or steal his ball from him," Alfredo continued.

Amy crossed past Alfredo so she could change the rein. She sat for two beats and then continued to rise and fall with Archie's steady stride.

"Another important thing to remember, so you don't get a penalty, is to never block the path of the player who last hit the ball. Never touch an opposing player or pony with your mallet, and any contact through bumping must be made between the pony's hip and shoulder. Oh, and you're only allowed to hook if you're on the side that your opponent is swinging on, or if you're directly in front or behind him."

Thankfully, since she had watched the match the week before, Amy could picture most of what Alfredo was telling her.

"I'll give you a copy of the USPA rules later," he said. "But what the rules can't teach you is tactics. Tactics are about anticipating where the ball is going next rather than chasing it all around the field and always playing catch-up."

Amy nodded. "What position will I be playing?"

"Number one," Alfredo replied. "The most experienced team players usually play two and three. You're the team's offensive player, kind of like in hockey. The idea is that you get first shot at the goal, and your team members behind you can get another shot if you miss."

"Where does the offensive part come in?" Amy asked.

"Against the other team's number three. If I tell you any more, none of it will stick, so how about some practical work?"

Amy nodded and trotted into the center. She held out her hand for the mallet.

"The first thing I'd like you to do to get used to the mallet is to ride around the ring, swinging it. Bring it in front of you, up in an arc, down in an arc, and swing it in complete circles until it feels like an extension of your arm."

Amy trotted Archie up the length of the arena, swinging the mallet until her arm started to ache. She almost dropped it when she tried for a full swing. Archie had kept up a steady pace, ignoring her lack of attention to her riding. "Thanks, boy," she said to the pony. When she turned Archie back down the arena, she squeezed him into a canter.

"Go again," Alfredo told her when she pulled up alongside him.

Amy kept on working the mallet and began to see what Alfredo meant about it becoming a natural extension of her arm. There was so much to concentrate on in a polo match that she couldn't afford to give her entire focus to the mallet.

"Now, when you canter down the line, I want you to hit the ball and aim for the posts," Alfredo said. He positioned the ball about twenty feet in front of the cones.

Amy cantered Archie up to the top of the arena and reined him around. She had to grab a handful of mane when he took her by surprise with the sharpness of his turn. *I'm going to have to be glued into the saddle come Friday,* Amy thought.

She focused entirely on the ball as they cantered down the arena. *One, two, three,* she counted Archie's strides to the target. With a quick glance at the cones to establish her line, Amy swung back the mallet and hit the ball. With a rush of delight she watched it scud between the cones.

"How much did you have to focus on the mallet just then?" Alfredo asked as she brought Archie to a halt.

"Hardly at all," Amy admitted.

"Good work," Alfredo told her. "What do you think about practicing on Impala this evening?" He reached up and rested his hand on Archie's neck. "If you're going to ride her on Friday, then the sooner you get used to her, the better."

"Sure." Amy nodded. "But I'd like to do another join-up with her before I ride."

Alfredo looked straight into Amy's eyes. "Do you think all this work with her will make a difference for Friday's match?"

"I'm sure it will," Amy told him. *But will it be enough of a difference?* she wondered.

❧

That evening, Amy and Alfredo led Impala and Palma into the arena. Both horses were fully tacked. Amy took Impala to the center of the arena and secured her reins through her throatlatch to stop them from trailing. "Off you go." She flicked her lead line at Impala's hindquarters.

Amy read the expression of surprise on the mare's face. She ran forward a few steps and then looked around uncertainly. "Go on, you know what to do," Amy said, flicking her again.

Impala broke into a trot and when Amy flicked the lead line just behind her hocks, Impala bucked and broke into a canter. She kept Impala running until the mare showed signs that she wanted to join up with her.

Amy became distracted by Papa and Jaime, walking down to the arena gate. Sensing her lack of attention, Impala began to slow her pace. Amy stepped forward and made the mare speed up again. It was important that she retain control of the join-up. Impala lowered her head and began to open and close her mouth.

"OK, girl," Amy murmured. "Time to come in."

She turned her back on, Impala and in just a few short moments the mare bumped her nose into Amy's back. Wherever she went, Impala followed, a faithful shadow. Amy turned and patted Impala's neck. "Well done," she whispered. She stroked the mare's nose and leaned close. "I'm going to ride you now, sweetheart. Just keep trusting me, OK?"

She pulled down Impala's stirrups and checked the girth before swinging up onto her back. Impala shifted her weight restlessly as she landed in the saddle. Feeling nervous, Amy nodded at Alfredo, who was already mounted on Palma. He rolled the ball down the centerline. In a shower of sand, he was suddenly cantering toward Amy and the mare.

"Whoa," Amy said as Impala ran backward.

"Race you to the ball!" Alfredo called.

Amy struggled to turn Impala around as she tried to run for the gate. "Come on, Impala," she urged. She drove the mare forward, not giving her a chance to have second thoughts.

Impala carried her head as high as the standing martingale would allow. She broke into a canter, moving sideways as she tried to evade Amy's hands. Amy sat deep to encourage Impala to straighten. "Remember our join-up, remember how you trusted me," she murmured.

She noticed Alfredo riding wide of the ball to give her and Impala the chance to take a hit. She tightened her grasp on the mallet as she persuaded Impala to near their target. Amy took a swing at the ball as they cantered past but she was concentrating so hard on not hitting Impala with the mallet that she missed. She reined Impala around and the mare responded, turning like a jackknife.

Alfredo had ridden a circle and was closing in on the ball from the opposite direction.

Impala shied away, unseating Amy. "Come on, girl, you can do this, I know it." Amy used her inside rein and outside leg, and Impala responded by lengthening her stride.

Alfredo and Palma were bearing down on the ball, and Amy leaned as far out of the saddle as she dared. Impala reached the ball half a stride before Palma, and Amy swung her mallet. She caught the ball and sent it scudding down the arena. As her mallet carried through the swing, Amy lost her balance. She made a grab at Impala's mane but the mare swerved away from underneath her. Amy fell through the air and desperately kicked her foot out of the stirrup iron. She tried to hold on to her reins but Impala reared and twisted them out of her reach. She fell hard on her side and could only watch as Impala galloped to the arena gate where Papa grabbed her reins. Amy closed her eyes and groaned.

"Are you OK?" Alfredo halted Palma and jumped down. He knelt beside her, his face clouded with worry.

"I'm fine," she told him. She tried to sit up but her chest felt as if all the air had been knocked out of it.

"Lie still for a moment," Alfredo urged. He gently unbuckled her chin strap and eased off her hat. "You need to catch your breath."

"I feel so dumb," Amy wheezed. "It wasn't Impala's fault. I leaned too far out of the saddle. She just got freaked out by my fall."

"I always knew your competitive streak would get you

in trouble!" Alfredo said. He leaned down to brush a strand of Amy's hair off her cheek.

She stared into his deep brown eyes.

Instead of straightening up, Alfredo held her gaze. "I'm sorry you got hurt," he murmured.

Amy suddenly felt tongue-tied. "I'm OK," she managed.

Alfredo slipped his arm around her waist and helped her to stand up.

She still felt a little weak but her breath had come back. "Thanks."

Alfredo took his arm away. "Sure." He reached up to take Palma's reins. The gelding had waited patiently beside them.

They headed down to the gate, and Amy steeled herself for whatever Papa would have to say.

"Are you OK?" Jaime asked. "You were doing great before you fell. Well done!"

"You are congratulating her for getting a trained polo pony to make one shoddy pass at a ball?" Papa sounded incredulous.

Amy took Impala's reins from Papa. "It's a breakthrough that she was prepared to get close to the ball even though there was another horse closing in on her. She should be rewarded for it." She met Papa's gaze and refused to look away.

Papa raised his eyebrows. "All this pandering to

the horse — you'll be spoon-feeding her oats next! At the rate she's going, she just might make *novice* level in the next five years."

"Papa," Alfredo spoke up. "Amy's way might not be your way, but she's Impala's last chance."

"I never thought I'd say this, but I'm starting to doubt you'll ever make a polo horse out of that one," Papa told him. "Either hand her over to a more experienced rider who might be able to make something of her, or get rid of her altogether, that's my advice."

Amy stared at Papa, feeling anger rising inside her. Didn't the old man know the effect his words could have on Alfredo?

Papa turned his back and headed to the house, picking his way carefully with his walking stick.

"You got her to close in on the ball, that's terrific," Jaime said, breaking the strained atmosphere. He leaned on the gate and looked Impala over. "And she's not showing her usual signs of stress. At the last match, she was wild-eyed and jumping all over the place."

Amy was grateful to Jaime for acting as if Papa hadn't spoken. He was right, Impala didn't feel bunched up and fearful. *But she still fought me for much of the practice. It's such a small step forward*, she thought.

"That was amazing, watching her follow you around the ring," Jaime added, reaching out with a horse cookie for Impala. He stroked Impala's cheek as the mare lipped the cookie off his hand.

"She responds really well to the join-up," Amy agreed. "She just wants to please and whatever it is that's making her freak out, she has no control over it, I'm sure."

Alfredo led Palma forward to open the gate. "That was a definite improvement," he said. "You're doing great, Amy."

But his voice was flat and he didn't meet her eyes. Amy got the feeling that Alfredo was more wounded by Papa's words than he was going to admit.

Chapter Eleven

The next day, Susannah offered to drive Amy into town to look for a cocktail dress for Friday's party. Amy pulled on a denim skirt and tank top in her room and put her hair in a low ponytail. She picked up her purse before heading outside, where Susannah was already waiting in an adorable red convertible.

"All set?" Susannah was wearing her hair in a sophisticated French twist. She put on a pair of fancy-looking sunglasses before turning the key in the ignition.

Amy fastened her seat belt as the car smoothly pulled away.

"This is going to be so much fun," Susannah said. "I have to practically drag Dacil and Celeste into town whenever they need an outfit."

"It seems the older I get, the more I like shopping," Amy admitted. "And I don't get too many chances to do it."

"You must be kept very busy between your studies and going home. Something tells me that you don't spend much time relaxing during your vacations."

"I love helping out when I'm home," Amy explained. She leaned back, enjoying the blowing wind as they drove.

"It must be difficult getting into the swing of things when you're only home on visits and not living there." Susannah slowed for the electronic gates to open.

It was true. It wasn't easy going home and figuring out how to fit in. It wasn't right to swoop in and take control, but it felt strange to wait for someone else to tell her what needed to be done. "I think we're starting to figure it out. Ty runs the yard now and he keeps me in the loop."

"It sounds like a delicate balance," Susannah said as the car accelerated onto the main road.

Balance, Amy mused: It was what her work was all about.

Susannah drove into East Hampton town. She parked and they walked down Main Street past a string of upscale stores and, judging by the names on the store windows, Amy could tell that these shops were exclusive. Buying a designer dress would probably blow her entire vacation budget. But then again, anything less than fabulous would look completely out of place at the polo party.

"Shall we try in here?" Susannah suggested, stopping outside a stylish boutique window featuring a pair of mannequins. "My friend Jacqueline says that her daughter raves about this place," Susannah explained, pushing open the door.

An assistant approached them. "Hi there," she said with a warm smile. "Are you looking for something specific?"

"We're looking for a cocktail dress," Susannah told her.

The assistant gave Amy a discerning look and began glancing around the store. After a moment, she moved pointedly to a rack and pulled out two dresses. One was black lace and the other was red with a fitted bodice and flared skirt. "I think these would look great on you. Would you like to try them?"

Susannah sat down on one of the cream-colored sofas underneath a chandelier while Amy followed the sales-woman to a changing room.

As soon as she was alone in the brightly lit cubicle, she checked the price tags. She caught her breath when she saw the cost of the dresses. *Well,* she thought, *how many chances will I have to buy a totally indulgent dress?*

She tried on the black lace dress first. It was fitted and short, but a square neckline gave it a sophisticated look.

Amy admired the matching lace collar and exquisite sheer fingerless gloves that the saleslady had grabbed to go with it.

The dress was so perfect that she almost didn't bother putting on the other one. She put the black dress back on its hanger and slipped on the red one. She was stunned when she looked in the mirror. Against her suntan, the color of the dress gave her an almost exotic look. The fitted bodice and soft flared skirt made her waist look tiny. She walked out of the changing room to show it to Susannah. "I thought the black at first, but now I'm not so sure."

Susannah looked up with a huge smile. "You look stunning! I'm not sure the young women at the party will forgive us for bringing you, because I'm sure every man's eyes will be on you!"

Amy felt herself blush as her thoughts immediately leaped to Alfredo. "Thanks. I'll just go get changed."

When she headed out of the room carrying the red dress, the sales assistant took it to be wrapped. "That is quite a dress," Susannah said.

Amy smiled. "It's a clear departure from my usual look!" She hesitated, but then decided to go ahead and ask what was on her mind. "Does Alfredo have a date for the dance?"

Susannah raised her eyebrows in surprise. "Hasn't he asked you?" Amy shook her head. "How like an Escobar man to just assume you'll be going with him." She winked.

"I guess he's got a lot on his mind at the moment," Amy said, noticing that the sales assistant had finished wrapping and boxing her dress. She went over to the register to pay.

"Mrs. Escobar has already settled the bill," the sales assistant told her as she handed Amy the box.

Amy felt sure that her jaw must have hit the floor. She hurried over to Susannah. "I couldn't . . ." she began.

"Please. Let me do this one small thing," Susannah said quietly, touching Amy's arm. "You are doing so much for us, and if it hadn't been for our invitation, you wouldn't have needed to buy a dress."

Amy thought of the total luxury she'd been living in for the last few days, and the warmth of the Escobars' hospitality. "Really, I'm not doing so much," she argued, "and you've already been so kind to me."

Susannah slipped her arm through Amy's. "Not only are you giving us your precious time and expertise, you've put a smile on Alfredo's face. That is something I haven't seen for most of the summer, and it's priceless. You've brought him hope, Amy."

The two of them left the store and made their way to a café. Susannah gestured to a table and they took a seat. "I'm afraid I'll let him down," Amy confessed. "I'm still not sure what's causing Impala's problems, so I can't treat her specifically. All I'm doing at the moment is giving her general treatment for fear, and hoping that keeping her away from other horses in the turnout paddock might be the answer." She paused as a waiter came by to take their order.

Susannah ordered two iced lattes and then turned her attention back to Amy. "Alfredo is sure that you're making headway with Impala already," she said warmly. "Before you came, he was convinced that it was all because of his weakness as a trainer and rider." She hesitated. "Papa means well, but he doesn't always say the most tactful things. Alfredo forever wants to live up to his grandfather, who has always been something of a hero to him. He worked so hard at his riding that he's been part of Pablo's team for nearly six years. He was one of the youngest players ever to make the professional circuit. But to feel he's earning Papa's disappointment this season has been crushing for him." She paused. "But then you came to help and believed that the problem is rooted in Impala's psyche. For the first time in months, Alfredo is beginning to believe in himself again."

Amy bit her lip. "Papa came down to the arena last night and told Alfredo to give up on Impala."

Susannah sighed. "Then let's just hope that Impala will respond to your treatment. Once Alfredo gets to ride her in a match without failure, it will be indisputable proof that he has every bit as much horse mastery running through his veins as the rest of the Escobars."

"Alfredo's lucky to have you," Amy said. "You understand him so well."

"Thank you," Susannah said. "I admit it hasn't always been easy. He was just five years old when his mother abandoned him. It took him a long time before he was able to trust another woman in his life."

Amy blinked in surprise. Slowly, the word *abandoned* sank in. "She walked out on Alfredo?"

Susannah looked sad. "Yes. She left without any explanation and never got back in touch. Not to find out how Alfredo was, or to send him a birthday or Christmas card. Nothing."

Amy was stunned. Suddenly, it became clear why nobody spoke about Alfredo's mother and why there wasn't a photograph of her anywhere in the house. She couldn't believe that any mother could be so callous. "Poor Alfredo," she whispered. "I'm so glad he has you now, and Celeste and Dacil."

Susannah nodded. "I often forget that they're not full siblings." She paused as the waiter arrived with their drinks. "Are you close with your family?"

Amy hesitated. "My mom died when I was fifteen but I'm very close to my grandpa and sister."

"So you went through most of your teenage years without your mother being around." Susannah's voice was full of compassion. "Is your sister younger or older than you?"

"Older," Amy told her. "Which sometimes helped and other times didn't." She smiled sadly.

Susannah chuckled.

As they sipped their drinks, Amy's thoughts returned to Alfredo. She understood how much he needed to prove his abilities, both to his family and himself, but she was beginning to have doubts about spending so much time training for the polo match. She should be putting all of her efforts into getting Alfredo and Impala together as a team. *He should be riding on Friday, not me,* she realized.

❧

That evening, Alfredo went down to the arena to school Palma, so Amy decided to go see Impala. The mare was alone in a paddock adjoining another, in which Alfredo's string was grazing. Amy leaned over the gate and watched the mare. Impala was close against the fence and every so often would call to the other horses. Amy's doubts increased. It didn't feel right that Impala was being bullied, not when she was clearly trying to get close to the herd.

"Impala!" she called.

Impala looked over and pricked her ears. She whickered when she saw Amy. Amy reached into her pocket for a horse cookie and held out her hand. "Come on, beautiful."

Impala halted a few feet away from Amy and reached to lip the treat off her hand, her soft muzzle grazing Amy's palm. As she crunched on the cookie, she stepped closer. "There's no more." Amy laughed, feeling Impala reach through the bars to nibble at her pocket. She climbed up onto the gate and ran her hand down Impala's muscular neck. "If only we could get you to enjoy polo, you would be truly awesome," she murmured, teasing a burr out of Impala's tufty forelock. She stroked the mare's soft cheek. "What are you so afraid of, huh?"

Impala gave a heavy sigh as if she wished Amy could read her mind.

"I do, too," Amy said, giving the mare a hug. "It would make things so much easier!"

❧

The following morning Alfredo brought Sotto and Archie down to the arena.

"Shouldn't I be riding Impala?" Amy said.

"Sotto's my most experienced horse. Training on him today will mean you don't have to worry about anything other than yourself," Alfredo told her.

Amy realized that it made sense. Alfredo mounted Archie and rode behind Amy to warm up. She trotted Sotto on one rein, and then the other, around the arena.

At fifteen hands three inches tall, the powerful black was bigger than any of Alfredo's other horses. His stride ate up the ground and he obeyed Amy's signals perfectly.

Once Sotto and Archie were warmed up, Alfredo threw the ball into the arena. "OK, that's your goal." He pointed to two cones set out at the top end of the arena. "Let's see how many points you can score." He cantered away and then turned to face her. "Go!"

The moment Amy turned Sotto toward the ball, the gelding put on a burst of speed that left her breathless. She leaned over Sotto's neck and concentrated on lining up her mallet with the ball. They reached the ball before Alfredo and Archie. As the opposite pair thundered toward them, Amy drew back her mallet. With a sharp crack, the ball flew down the arena and she urged Sotto forward.

She was aware of Alfredo circling and chasing after them. With a thrill of exhilaration, she hit the ball a second time, aiming at the goal. The ball scudded over the ground and bounced between the cones.

"Yeah!" she yelled. She leaned forward to pat Sotto's shoulder. "Good boy!"

"Best of three," Alfredo called, hitting the ball toward his end of the arena.

Like he'd been released from a slingshot, Sotto launched forward as soon as Amy gave him the signal.

When they reached the ball, Amy hit it backward and then turned Sotto around. As she chased after the ball once more, she saw Alfredo take a swing and send it between the posts.

"Lucky shot," she called to him.

She got the ball and hit it down the field. Alfredo and Archie matched Sotto and Amy stride for stride as they galloped down the arena. As Alfredo raised his mallet to hit the ball back, Amy lifted her mallet to block him. She managed to hit the ball toward her own goal and whooped as the ball rolled between the cones. She turned Sotto and waved her mallet in the air. "I think that makes it two to one."

"*I* think you'll find that makes you ready for the match on Friday," Alfredo called.

Amy slowed Sotto and pulled up beside Alfredo. "You really think so?"

"You're a fast learner," he told her. He pulled out of his stirrups and jumped down.

"Well, coming from you, I'll take that as a compliment," Amy said as she dismounted.

🙞

Amy checked with Chrissie before turning Impala out that evening, and after she had massaged lavender oil into Impala's coat, she slipped on the mare's summer sheet. "Are you ready to go out?"

Impala gave Amy's shoulder a friendly nudge. Amy clipped on the lead rope and slid back the stall door. She walked Impala out of the yard and down the path. When they reached the first paddock, Impala stopped and let out a piercing neigh. Palma and Sotto, who were grazing near the gate, trotted toward them. Sotto stretched his neck over the gate to Impala and the mare strained against the lead rope. Amy hesitated and then pulled back the clasp on the gate. The more she got to know Impala, the more she doubted the mare was being bullied by her herd. "Go on," she said, and slipped off Impala's halter.

With a snort, Impala cantered into the field. Amy held her breath as Sotto and Palma turned and chased after her. Impala wheeled around and skidded to a halt. Amy's fingers tightened on the gate. Had she done the wrong thing?

Sotto reached out and, to Amy's relief, he began to groom Impala gently with his teeth. Palma dropped his head down to graze beside her, keeping close. Watching the reunion, Amy knew that her original diagnosis had been wrong. Impala was clearly happy to be back with her herd in the field. Amy leaned her forearms on the gate and decided to hang around for a while longer to check that the mare truly was okay.

Impala and Sotto stopped grooming each other and dropped their heads to graze. Amy stared at their dark shapes silhouetted against the orange-and-red backdrop of the setting sun. *It's great that she's not being bullied, but I now have absolutely no idea what's making her play-up on the polo field*, she thought.

"That's not a horse that looks bullied to me." Papa's voice broke in on Amy's thoughts as he came to stand beside her.

"No," Amy admitted. She tensed, waiting for Papa's scathing response. When it didn't come, she glanced at the old man and saw him watching Impala, his eyebrows furrowed. "We should have called her Enigma instead of Impala," he murmured.

"She certainly is a mystery," Amy agreed. "But I don't believe that any horse misbehaves without reason."

"Pah! All this psychoanalysis mumbo jumbo! The simple fact is that the horse doesn't have what it takes. If she'd been put into the hands of a more experienced rider, then maybe she would have turned out differently. But you saw Alfredo's reaction to my suggestion that Pablo take on Impala." He shrugged. "It's time to give up before Team Escobar becomes a laughing-stock."

"Don't you think you're being hard on Alfredo?" Amy couldn't help challenging him. She turned to face Papa. "I haven't heard you compliment him once in all the time I've been here. Not even after his match when he played so well. I don't think there are many riders who could have stayed on Impala or persuaded her to stay on the pitch."

"She was only on the pitch for seven minutes," Papa said dismissively. "And it looked more like a rodeo performance. Is this what I built up the Escobar reputation for? So my grandson and a mare, who can trace her ancestry back to Manticore, can blow everything in a single season? It is a shame to me!"

"The shame is in making Alfredo feel that he'll never live up to you or your name no matter how good he is!" Amy said sharply.

The old man's eyes widened in surprise.

"I'm sorry," Amy apologized. "I didn't mean to be rude, but can't you see how much Alfredo is up against?"

Papa's color had darkened. "What? What do you think he has to work against?" he demanded. "The boy has the best of everything! When I was his age I was working a fifteen-hour day. What does he know of getting up at five A.M. each morning?"

"But he has so much to live up to," Amy said. "You were amazingly successful in your career and he is constantly reminded of that by pictures and medals and trophies." She took a deep breath. "And with his mother walking out on him at such an early age, I'm sure Alfredo blamed himself. Maybe he feels he wasn't good enough to make her want to stay. And now he's not good enough for you, either."

"What do you know of that?" Papa scowled. "The best thing that woman did was to leave. She never understood our tradition. She never attended a match, and gave no support to Pablo's career. I don't know why he married her in the first place."

"All I know is that as a child, Alfredo probably blamed himself, not her," Amy said quietly. "It took me a long time to stop feeling guilty after my mom died." She sighed. "Not having your mother around affects you every day. At least I know what happened to my mother, and she's gone. It must be so much harder for Alfredo, knowing that she's out there somewhere and doesn't want anything to do with him."

Papa turned and stared at the horizon. He didn't speak for a long time.

Just as Amy decided it would be better if she left, Papa cleared his throat.

"She did try to contact him. Every birthday and Christmas she would send a card. But it was better that she was out of his life altogether. She never did any good when she was in it. How could she do any good once she had left?"

Amy was horrified. What right did he have to keep Alfredo's mother from getting in touch with her son?

Papa had let Alfredo believe that the most important person in his life had abandoned him when he was just a child.

Papa continued, still gazing over the fence. "Then Susannah came and made the house and everyone in it happier than ever before. I didn't want anything to get in the way. I watched Alfredo forget his own mother and love Susannah as if she were his real parent." His voice caught. "Now here you are telling me that he never forgot her? He thinks of her every day?"

"I can only tell you how *I* feel," Amy said. She realized that Papa had tried to act in Alfredo's best interests, even if what he had done had been entirely wrong. "Alfredo will never forget his real mother, however much he loves Susannah."

She decided to give Papa some time on his own. The conversation had given him much to think about. But with this new insight, Amy realized that she might be able to figure out what was wrong with Impala after all.

Chapter Twelve

❧

Amy went down for breakfast early the next morning. She and Alfredo had arranged another training session. Alfredo walked in just as Amy was helping herself to orange juice and fresh melon. The enormity of Papa's secret loomed between them and Amy couldn't meet Alfredo's eyes. Eventually, she managed to push her conversation with Papa to the back of her mind and force herself to look at Alfredo.

"Are you ready for some hard work?" Alfredo asked, his eyes twinkling.

"Just as soon as I can wake up." Amy pretended to groan.

"I thought you could ride each of my string today for seven minutes each. That's the length of time you'll be on them tomorrow for each chukker," Alfredo said as he poured himself some coffee. "I asked Chrissie to get them tacked up."

Amy got her own coffee and wondered if she should discuss her thoughts about Impala's behavior with Alfredo now. *No*, she thought. *I'll wait until we're down on the yard.*

"Are you okay? Are you nervous?" Alfredo looked at her with concern.

"I guess." Amy decided to allow Alfredo to think it was nerves affecting her. "I can't believe I agreed to play in a match tomorrow!"

"Juan's coming over tonight. I thought I could arrange for him, Jaime, and Dad to ride with us this evening so you could experience playing with a group. Maybe then it will sink in." He smiled.

Amy scraped up the last of her breakfast. "Sounds like a plan." She couldn't help feeling uneasy about riding the next day. If she did ride Impala and the mare turned in a good performance, Alfredo would be even more convinced that his riding was weak. *But if Alfredo rides tomorrow and Impala misbehaves, it will be yet another bad experience. I'm not sure how many more he can take without throwing in the towel,* she considered.

As they walked down to the barn, she longed to tell Alfredo that she knew about what had happened with his mother. She had spent so much time getting to know Impala, but she needed to have the same sense of closeness with the rider, too. Especially because she was starting to think that the problem was one that they shared. . . .

Alfredo shot her a sideways glance as if he were trying to tune in to her thoughts. But then he looked away and thrust his hands into the pockets of his yard jacket. "Let's start with Sotto," Alfredo said.

"How about we do T-touch on Impala before we train?" Amy suggested.

"You're still doing that?"

"Every morning," Amy replied.

As they headed toward Impala's stall, Chrissie met them, carrying an armful of tack. "I'll get Impala ready last so you have plenty of time to see to her," she told them before letting herself into Archie's stall.

Impala was looking through her door. The moment she saw Amy, she lifted her head and gave a low whicker of welcome.

Alfredo looked surprised. "She never does that for me!" He rubbed Impala's nose. "Maybe I should start bringing you some horse cookies!"

Amy looked at the way Alfredo was fussing over Impala and knew that he would think her latest diagnosis of Impala was crazy. But she had to tell him, no matter how hard it would be for him to hear. She took a deep breath. "I think you're going to need more than horse cookies."

Alfredo frowned. "Huh? Is this about Impala's behavior?" He looked confused.

"I think so." Amy nodded. "Impala loves you, there's no doubt about that. But love is very different from trust. How do you feel about working on trust with Impala today?"

Alfredo shook his head. "There's no need. No one knows Impala better than I do. From the moment she was born, I've been in charge of her."

"I know," Amy said quickly. "I'm not questioning your dedication. In fact, I never thought that there was a problem in your relationship with Impala because you're so committed to her."

Alfredo's eyes widened. "Are you saying that you changed your mind?"

Amy felt her stomach twist. "Your relationship is built on the mechanics of riding and handling. It's not based on care. When Impala's cold, who gives her a warm rug? When Impala's hungry, who feeds her? When she's sick, who nurses her? Who gives her a clean bed to sleep in?"

"I don't do those things for any of my other horses," Alfredo pointed out, "but they don't act up on me. You're wrong, Amy, again." His eyes were dark with accusation.

Impala threw her head up at the note of anger in his voice. She backed away until there was a clear distance between them.

Amy felt her cheeks burn. Papa had obviously told Alfredo that she'd admitted to being wrong about Impala being bullied. "Impala is different from your other horses," she said quietly. "Look at the way she's responding to us arguing. She's one of the most sensitive horses I've ever known. I think it's hard for her to trust, and she needs to have total trust in her rider before she'll give her all. Joining up with her is one of the most effective ways of gaining her trust. It's why she called out to me when she saw me today."

"But when you rode her after your join-up, she didn't behave perfectly for you," Alfredo pointed out.

Amy nodded. "I think she was picking up on *my* insecurities. I was unsure of the polo maneuvers and Impala needs a supremely confident rider." She hesitated. "Instead of training me this morning, I think you should join up with Impala. And I don't think that I should ride in tomorrow's match. I think you should."

Alfredo stared at her. "Are you backing out because you're scared of riding her?"

Amy shook her head. "It's true that I don't think a novice polo rider will do Impala any favors, but the reason I want you to ride is because I really believe that if you develop a deeper bond with her through a join-up, she'll give her heart and soul for you on the pitch tomorrow."

Alfredo turned away and slipped one arm around Impala. "I don't want to believe that will happen if I'm just going to be disappointed." He pressed his face into Impala's neck.

Amy's heart went out to Alfredo. He had faced rejection and disappointment so many times. It was no wonder he was scared to take another risk. "I know the pressure you must feel living up to the Escobar tradition," she said softly. "But you need to focus on you and Impala. Succeed for her and succeed for you, not anyone else."

Alfredo shook his head. "You don't understand."

"I do," Amy said, feeling her eyes sting. "My mother died when I was fifteen. It was only after she died that I began to understand the importance of what she had done with her life and I began to learn it for myself. But no matter how many times I help a horse by using her methods, I'll never stop longing to have her standing beside me, reassuring me." Her voice broke and she looked down at the ground. The straw turned into a yellow blur before her eyes.

She suddenly felt Alfredo's arms around her. "I'm sorry," he murmured against her hair. "I'm so sorry."

"My mom left me when I was five," he went on, not realizing Amy already knew. "She never contacted me again. She never picked up the phone to see how I was.

At my first day of school, everyone else had their moms come to get them. I tried to pretend I didn't care that I didn't have a mom holding out her arms to me as I came running out the door." He gave a short harsh laugh. "It's the small things you remember, like not having anyone to write a Mother's Day card for, when all the other kids did. When I got sick, my dad would read me stories and make me hot chocolate. It wasn't his fault, but all I really wanted was my mom." His voice cracked.

Amy put her arms around him and felt her tears scald her cheeks. "I'm sorry, too," she whispered. She longed to tell Alfredo that his mother hadn't truly abandoned him. Yes, she'd left the Escobar home, and Amy would never understand why she hadn't taken Alfredo with her. *But she had wanted a relationship with him. If it hadn't been for Papa, who knows what might have been?* she thought.

They held each other for a long time before Amy finally pulled away. She might not be able to change what happened in Alfredo's past, but she could help his present situation. "I think that you're caught in a vicious circle," she told Alfredo as she wiped her eyes. "The more Impala acts up, the more you feel the pressure of not living up to the Escobar tradition of success. The more you feel the pressure, the more tense you are and the more Impala acts up."

"That makes sense," he admitted.

"We need to break the circle now," Amy said. "You need to join up with Impala so she can start trusting you enough to take part in the most scary of situations."

Alfredo took a deep breath. "OK," he said. "Let's give it a try."

▬

Amy went to tell Chrissie not to tack up the rest of Alfredo's horses. "We're going to work with just Impala instead."

Chrissie stared at her curiously. "Are you OK?"

"Fine, thanks, maybe a touch of allergies," Amy said, realizing her eyes must be red. "See you later."

"Later," Chrissie echoed.

Amy walked down to the arena with Alfredo and Impala without speaking. She felt drained by their emotional exchange and figured Alfredo felt the same.

They led Impala into the middle of the arena. "I'm sorry I let you down," Alfredo murmured to the mare. "But this is where it stops."

Impala nibbled at his collar. It was clear that the pair of them didn't need a bond to be created, but they did need their existing bond to be deepened.

"Now send her away," Amy told Alfredo.

Alfredo hesitated. "It was OK for you to drive her off because she didn't know you. She's going to be totally confused if I do it."

Amy placed her hand on Alfredo's arm. "Please, Alfredo, trust me." She could feel how tense he was. "Believe me, this will make your bond with Impala even stronger. It will strengthen her faith in you because what she will remember is what happens at the end of the join-up. She'll ask to be accepted by you and you'll agree," Amy reassured him.

She unsnapped Impala's lead rope and handed it to Alfredo.

Alfredo took the lead rein and hesitated. Amy gently placed her hand over his and moved it so that the end of the rein flicked against Impala's hindquarters.

Impala snorted in surprise and shied away.

"Again," Amy urged, taking her hand away.

This time when Alfredo flicked the rein, Impala broke into a canter and sought the security of the fence.

"That's great," Amy told him. "Keep her running until she begins to tell you that she wants to place her trust in you as the stronger partner."

After a few circuits Impala lowered her head.

"Now, step forward," Amy told Alfredo.

Alfredo took a step so he was in line with Impala's head. He broke into a smile as the mare immediately responded by slowing down. Before Amy could prompt him, Alfredo took a step back. Impala put on a spurt of speed, thinking that he was going to chase her again.

"She's totally focused on me," Alfredo said with a note of awe in his voice.

Amy nodded. "Her inside eye and ear are fixed on your every move."

Impala's tail streamed like a banner as she flew across the ground with her long strides. The morning sun turned her coat to burnished bronze.

Impala lowered her head to the ground and began opening and closing her mouth. "That's the sign I'm waiting for, right?" Alfredo asked.

"She's showing you she doesn't want to run away from you anymore," Amy said softly. "She's saying that she wants to place her trust in you because she knows you'll protect her."

She waited a few moments more. "Now," she said, "turn your back on her so that she knows she has nothing to fear from you."

Alfredo slowly turned away.

Amy watched as Impala halted and looked at Alfredo. The horse whickered softly to him.

"Don't turn around," Amy murmured. "Let her come to you."

Impala left the track and began to walk toward Alfredo. Her hooves thudded over the sand. When she reached Alfredo, she nuzzled his shoulder.

"Walk forward," Amy whispered. "Show her that she's safe to follow wherever you lead."

Alfredo took three steps forward and waited. Impala followed him around the arena, patiently waiting whenever he stopped. Finally, Alfredo turned and slipped his arms around Impala's neck.

Amy caught her breath as she looked at Impala's face. The mare didn't need to talk. The relief in her eyes expressed trust and understanding with Alfredo that transcended any language.

Alfredo turned to look at Amy. "Thank you," he said simply.

Chapter Thirteen

❧

That night, supper was served on the patio under a trellis roof thick with roses. Juan had driven up from the city, which made ten of them sitting around the table.

Pablo clinked his fork against his glass. "I think it's time we all wished Amy the very best of luck tomorrow as an honorary member of Team Escobar!"

Alfredo cleared his throat. "There's been a change of plans. Amy's not riding after all." He glanced at Amy. "I am."

Pablo's eyebrows shot up in surprise. "Is that a good idea? You were rather, uh, emotional, after our last match. I think it's best that we look for a replacement for Impala before your next match. Tomorrow is only a scrimmage, after all. Let Amy play."

Amy's grip tightened on her cutlery. Unwittingly, Pablo was giving Alfredo yet another rejection.

"I'm sure Alfredo and Amy wouldn't have swapped arrangements unless they were sure of what they were doing," Susannah said. "Amy?"

Amy set down her knife and fork and glanced around the table. No one was eating. They were all waiting to hear her explanation, even Celeste and Dacil. More than ever she felt the weight of the Escobars' expectations. "Working with Impala has been like putting together a jigsaw puzzle and it's taken a while for all the pieces to fall into place. When I rode Impala on my first day here, she shied at a tree trunk. She thought it was a monster ready to pounce." Dacil gave a small giggle. Amy smiled at her and then continued. "She wasn't trying to be difficult. She was genuinely scared and that gave me my first clue — even though I didn't know it at the time."

Papa threw his napkin down on the table. "You've already jumped to one wrong conclusion. Impala wasn't being bullied. How are we to know that you aren't wrong again?"

"I suggested that Impala might be bullied because there didn't seem to be any other possible explanation for her behavior," Amy said, keeping her voice calm.

"And now?" Susannah prompted.

"Emotionally, she's something of a baby. She needs to be able to trust her rider and absorb confidence from that person." She broke off and glanced at Alfredo, not wanting to announce that his bond of trust hadn't been deep enough with Impala.

"But after you joined up with Impala she still acted up, and that's all about gaining trust, right?" Jaime said as he broke off the end of a bread stick and started munching on it thoughtfully.

"Yes, Alfredo pointed that out, too," she agreed. "Looking back, I can see that it was because I was inexperienced at polo. At the time I assumed her behavior couldn't be linked to a lack of trust, because, as you say, she misbehaved after we had joined up. I could also see that there was a bond between Impala and Alfredo, so I didn't think that trust was the issue. His dedication to her was clear and so was her obvious desire to do her best for him. But it's been her fear of the noise and action of the game making her misbehave. She hasn't been able to overcome it because she didn't have enough confidence in Alfredo."

"So you're saying that is due to a lack of trust between her and Alfredo?" Papa sounded as incredulous as Alfredo had earlier.

"It wasn't Alfredo's fault," Amy said quickly. "Like I said, because of Impala's nature, she needs a deeper bond of trust with her rider than the average horse. Training and riding weren't enough to form that. But I believe the join-up today with Alfredo did." She didn't add that Alfredo had his own problems with trust, after spending most of his life believing that his mother had abandoned him.

"You did the same thing that we watched Amy do the other day?" Jaime asked Alfredo, looking impressed.

Alfredo nodded. "It was amazing," he said, meeting Amy's eyes and sharing a smile with her.

"I saw Amy join up with Impala the other day and believe me, there's a lot to it. It's something I'd like to learn more about," Pablo said thoughtfully. He looked at Alfredo. "So you and Impala joined up today and now you feel more confident about riding her tomorrow?"

"Yes," Alfredo replied. "To be honest, I was full of doubt before the join-up, but something changed afterward. It's hard to explain, but it's like I really know Impala now."

And you let her trust you, Amy thought.

Juan ran his hands through his hair. "I find it hard to believe that after one session this afternoon, our entire summer of problems with Impala is going to disappear." He shot Alfredo an apologetic look. "I'm not happy about you riding her tomorrow. Her performance at the last match and your reaction to it was the last straw as far as I'm concerned. I think it's time we called it a day."

Alfredo's color darkened. Amy guessed for one horrifying moment that he thought he was losing his place on the team. "I see," he said.

"It's my call and I trust Alfredo's judgment," Pablo cut in firmly. "We'll give Impala one more try." He hesitated. "But if she does act up tomorrow, then I'm afraid we will have to replace her on the team. Our handicap is starting to become affected by her performance."

Alfredo leaned over and shook his father's hand. "Agreed."

☙

After the meal, Amy decided to slip outside for a walk. It had been an incredibly draining day. She sat out by the pool for a while watching the moon play on the water. She got up and walked away from the pool and around the house to the main lawn. Subtle lighting in the shrubbery marked the path, but she could have found her way by the full moon, it shone so brightly.

Amy thought of what Alfredo had faced that day. He needed to trust Impala, and let her trust him in return. He came from a loving, warm family and his relationship with his stepmother couldn't be stronger, but his childhood had been scarred by the loss of the person who mattered most. She longed to tell him that his mother hadn't totally rejected him, but she knew the truth had to come from Papa. Amy felt a sharp jab of pain that her own mother was beyond all reach. The closest she could come to a relationship with her mom was by continuing her work with horses.

She wandered down to the paddocks, suddenly feeling the need to be with Impala. But as she drew closer to the field she noticed that someone else was already there. Amy peered at the person's silhouette and realized it was Alfredo. He was sitting on the top rail speaking to Impala and she had her head resting on his shoulder. "I'm going to be there every step of the way tomorrow," Amy heard him say. "There's no need for you to be scared of anything, OK? I won't let you get hurt, I promise."

Amy backed away, unwilling to intrude. But as she headed back to the house, her heart felt lighter. It was clear that Alfredo and Impala had turned a corner. Tomorrow would be the first time that they would ride out as a real team.

❧

Back at the house, Amy was just heading up the stairs to bed when she heard her name called. She turned to see Papa standing in the hall. "I'd like to speak with you." Without waiting, he turned and walked into the living room.

Amy went in after him.

She found Papa standing underneath Manticore's painting. "Sit." He waved his hand toward a sofa.

Amy hoped that he wasn't looking for another confrontation. "So, you think you have solved the problem now, huh?" he said mildly.

"I hope that things are looking up for Alfredo and Impala," she replied. She hesitated. "Alfredo still has issues to work through, but you'll help him through those far better than I can."

Papa narrowed his eyes. "You blame me for what I did?"

"I think you did what you thought was best for your family because you love them very much," Amy said softly.

To her amazement, Papa's eyes filled with tears. "It's true what Alfredo says. You do read minds." He turned away, and Amy wondered if he was annoyed that he had shown her his vulnerability.

"It's not hard to see how much you love your family."

"I'm very proud of them, too," he said, and sighed deeply. "But I don't always show it enough."

"That's something you can work on," Amy said cautiously.

Papa scowled. "And I suppose you have more advice about Alfredo's mother, too!" he growled.

Amy realized that it was his way of asking her opinion, and suddenly, she wasn't afraid of him. "I think Alfredo is mature enough and wise enough to understand why you acted the way you did. I'm not saying he won't be angry and upset, but I think it's more important that he realizes his mother didn't totally abandon him. Don't you?"

Papa lowered himself onto the sofa. "The letters stopped arriving three years ago. I have no idea where Alfredo's mother lives now. What if he wants to seek her out?"

"Did you keep the old letters?" Amy asked.

Papa nodded.

"Then I'm sure he can trace her from the address on them. And since she never tried to hide herself away, it won't be too hard for him to track her down."

Papa nodded. "I'll think about it," he said.

Amy stood up, sensing their conversation was at an end. "I'll see you tomorrow."

Papa waved his hand to dismiss Amy but she didn't let the gesture bother her. She left the old man alone with his thoughts.

❧

"Hey, you beat me down here." Amy slid back the door to Impala's stall where Alfredo was busy massaging Impala's coat.

"I thought it would be a good idea to spend some time with her before the match. I've been using some of the lavender oil the way you showed me."

Amy was delighted that he was taking time to be with the mare. "How does she seem?" she asked. "The last match day, she was picking up on all the preparations and getting pretty tense."

"So far she seems fine," he said, patting Impala's neck. "She's eaten all her breakfast and she was happy to be cross-tied out in the aisle while Chrissie and I shampooed her."

"That's great," Amy said. She rubbed Impala's nose. "I'm sure she's going to do much better for you today."

"Hey, guys." Juan looked through the bars. "What are you doing, Alfredo?"

"It's called T-touch," Alfredo told him. "It's to help relax Impala."

Juan looked doubtful. "Do you think a match day is the best time to be changing your routine?"

"If I didn't think it was, then I wouldn't be doing it," Alfredo said defensively.

"I've been using T-touch on Impala each morning since I arrived, so it's not new to her," Amy added.

"Well, at least it's just a scrimmage today," Juan said, and shrugged. "If she does her whole split-personality thing on the field, it won't hurt us too much." He raised his hand. "I'll see you at breakfast."

Amy put her hand on Alfredo's arm. "Don't doubt yourself."

He scuffed the floor with his boot. "You heard my father yesterday. If Impala doesn't come through today, he's going to get rid of her." He looked up to meet Amy's gaze. "I don't want to lose her, Amy."

"I know," Amy said softly. "I know."

🙟

Still feeling troubled by the prospect of Impala losing her place in Alfredo's string, Amy went up to her room to get changed. She had left her laptop open and, glancing at the screen, she saw that she had two new messages, one from Ty and the other from Soraya.

She opened Ty's message first.

Hey, Amy.

The remedies you're giving Impala sound just right and it makes sense that she might be being bullied. My only other suggestion for you is to focus on Impala's relationship with her rider. He's the one riding her on the pitch when she freaks out and so maybe there's something there that needs working on. I know you're joining up with Impala, but maybe Alfredo should join up with her, too.

Good luck and give me a call if you need to talk things through.

(Sundance and Spindle say hi!)

Ty

Amy read Ty's confirmation of her diagnosis a second time. Being removed from the situation seemed to give him a clarity it had taken a while for her to find. She had been thrown off by Alfredo's dedication to Impala. She bit her lip. Now she only hoped that Alfredo trusted himself enough. She knew if he was insecure during the match, Impala was going to pick up on it and misbehave.

She sighed and clicked to open her other mail.

Hey, A.

Gotta keep this short. You know that I'm going to tell you to go for it with Alfredo! Have some fun! It's SUMMER!

I'm sure you're going to look fabulous tonight. Enjoy it and knock Alfredo's socks off.

XOXO

S

Amy smiled. Soraya's course in performing arts kept on spilling over into her conversation. Knock his socks off? But she couldn't help hoping Alfredo would be a little impressed by her fantastic new dress.

Just then, there was a knock on her door. "Come in," she called.

Papa walked into the room. "Do you have a moment?"

"Sure," Amy said, and watched as he made his way over to the easy chair and sat down.

"I want you to know that I've been doing much thinking since our conversation," Papa told her, leaning forward on his stick. "And I want to thank you for opening an old man's eyes."

Amy was amazed to hear Papa say that.

She hesitated before saying what was on her mind. "A wall's gone up between the two of you. I think you both need to be more honest with each other."

Papa waved his hand. "You're trying to spare my feelings. The wall is there because of my stubbornness and pride. I always think my way is the right way." The corners of his mouth tugged up. "I'm sure you needed me to point that out to you."

"Thank you," Amy said, unable to hold back a smile.

"I let Alfredo think he could never be good enough for Team Escobar, even though every time I see him in the saddle I'm filled with pride." Papa's hands trembled on his stick. "His mother was probably running away from the pressures of this family. She never felt that she fit in."

"Will you tell him about the letters?" Amy asked, holding her breath in anticipation of his answer.

He sighed. "I have no choice. I can't live with the knowledge that my actions are hurting him. I'll tell him soon. But today is going to be an Escobar victory that I don't want to spoil."

Amy went over and covered Papa's hands with her

own. "Before the match, will you at least let him know how proud you are of him and how much you believe in him? At the moment, he's going to ride out on that field believing that you're expecting him to fail."

Papa shook his head. "No. Failure isn't in his genes."

Amy caught the twinkle in his dark eyes and suddenly she saw how alike he and Alfredo were. She leaned down and kissed his cheek. "Then go tell him that."

Chapter Fourteen

❧

Amy felt a knot form in her stomach as she took her seat alongside the polo field. Dacil and Celeste were on one side of her, and Susannah was on the other, but Amy couldn't tune in to their chatter. She knew she wouldn't be able to relax until Alfredo had ridden Impala, and she hoped that Alfredo was feeling less anxious than she was. Impala would need Alfredo to be calm and focused. If she picked up on any tension from him, then the join-up would have little effect.

She felt Susannah squeeze her arm. "Are you OK?"

Amy gave a small smile. "I don't look OK?"

"He'll be fine," Susannah reassured her.

"I think I'll miss Impala going nuts on the pitch. It's the most interesting part of the match," Dacil commented.

"Dacil," Susannah said reprovingly.

"They're riding in!" Celeste interrupted.

Amy straightened in her seat as the teams cantered onto the pitch. She looked for Alfredo's number one shirt and saw that he was on Sotto. She understood why he would be first out on the powerful, experienced horse. Sotto would be confident and get Alfredo off to a good start.

The umpire threw in the ball, and Amy's heart quickened as the horses thundered down the field. Sotto appeared to fly as he and Alfredo worked their way to the front of the field, gaining on the ball. Alfredo raised his mallet as they flashed past Amy's seat, his gaze fixed on the ball. One of the players on the other team suddenly put on a burst of speed and gained on Sotto, riding up close and bumping Alfredo off the line of play. In a split second, the ball was stolen. The direction of play turned around, and Amy raised her binoculars as the horses galloped down the field. She couldn't see where the ball was until the other team's number one player swung his mallet making it shoot out from the pack of horses and scud off to the side of the goal.

"He was never going to make that, his angle was all wrong," Celeste said scornfully.

When the end of the first chukker sounded, neither team had scored. As the teams went to change horses, Amy felt her stomach twist with anxiety. Part of her wanted Alfredo to ride Impala and the other part of her wanted him to put it off for as long as possible.

She fidgeted and looked up as the crowd began to applaud. Alfredo was riding onto the pitch on a striking-looking chestnut with a bright star on her forehead. *Impala.*

Susannah reached for Amy's hand.

Amy squeezed Susannah's hand in return and then lifted her binoculars so she could closely examine Impala and Alfredo. Alfredo was sitting deep and his hands were relaxed on the reins, but Impala's tail was down, and Amy could read tension in her neck.

The play moved down the field, and as Alfredo sent Impala forward, the mare laid her ears flat and ran back.

"Come on, Impala," Amy urged.

Alfredo ran his gloved hand down her neck and then asked her to go again. After a moment's hesitation, Impala's ears pricked forward and, in an explosion of speed, she took off down the field. *She loves to run,* Amy thought, noting Impala's fluid stride and raised tail. But as Impala drew close to the players, her stride shortened and she fought Alfredo's hands, shaking her head in protest.

Amy felt her chest tighten. *Please, Impala, trust Alfredo.*

As the other team's number two raised his mallet to swing at the ball, Alfredo cut into the pack and leaned forward to hook the player. Impala's ears were back but she kept her position as Alfredo blocked the shot and hit the ball back.

Juan took up the play, reining Phoenix around sharply to head in the opposite direction toward the goal.

Amy looked back at Impala and gasped at the sharpness of her turn. It looked as if her legs would go out from under her. But Impala surged ahead of the other horses and Juan moved off the ball for Alfredo to take his place. Alfredo swung his mallet down and sent the ball soaring through the air. Impala stretched her neck out and left the other players behind as she galloped after the ball. Her burst of speed was incredible, but as they came to the ball, Alfredo asked her to slow and Impala obeyed.

Amy caught her breath as Alfredo swung his mallet. *Please, please go in.* The ball flew between the posts.

Amy and Susannah jumped to their feet and hugged each other. "It's wonderful!" Susannah said with a gasp.

Amy nodded and looked back at Alfredo and Impala. As the Escobar supporters cheered, Impala half bucked out of high spirits. *She's actually enjoying herself,* Amy realized with a surge of joy.

Alfredo was cantering up the field. As he rode past, he touched the handle of his mallet to his helmet in a salute to Amy.

For the first time that morning, she relaxed. It was hard to think that just a few minutes were all it had taken to turn both Alfredo's and Impala's lives around. Impala's future with the Escobars felt secure. Amy experienced a rush of joy for her friend, tinged with sadness that her time in the Hamptons was over. There was no need for her to stay with the Escobars any longer.

🙟

"Well done, Alfredo," Celeste cried as Alfredo appeared among the spectators who were milling about and socializing now that the match was over.

Alfredo swung his little sister into his arms. "Not bad, eh?" His eyes met Amy's. "I can't believe it," he told her. "It's all because of you. I don't know what to say."

Amy shook her head. "The victory is yours."

"Don't tell him that, he'll be even more impossible to live with." Dacil grinned.

Alfredo's eyes twinkled as he took a playful swipe at his sister. "I need to go see to Impala," he told Amy. "I want to wash her down. But I wanted to thank you first."

"I'll see you later," Amy promised, delighted that Alfredo's focus was on the comfort of his mare in spite of the staff that would take care of her without him.

"Later," Alfredo echoed.

Once they'd congratulated the rest of the team, Susannah drove Amy and the girls home so they would have plenty of time to get ready for the party that evening. Amy took a bubble bath and made time to polish her nails before getting dressed.

As she sat down at her dressing table to dry her hair, she felt a surge of panic. "Oh, no!" She set the dryer down and hurried over to her wardrobe. *What am I going to do for shoes?* she cried silently.

The only shoes she'd brought with her were her riding boots, some flip-flops, and a pair of sneakers.

She looked at the beautiful red dress and couldn't decide which set of shoes would look the least ridiculous. Amy didn't know whether to laugh or cry. Her only hope was that Susannah might be able to loan her a pair. She sat back down at the dressing table to finish drying her hair but she couldn't shake the disappointment that she wasn't going to look as perfect that night as she'd hoped. She tried not to think about it by focusing on what she could do with her hair. But her thoughts were interrupted by a tap on her shoulder.

"I hope you don't mind me coming in. You couldn't hear me knock over the dryer," Susannah explained.

"Of course not." Amy smiled, and switched it off. "I was about to come and find you . . ." She broke off as she noticed two boxes on her bed.

"You're going to think I'm a terrible meddler, but I thought you might not have any accessories for the dress," Susannah told her. "I was in town yesterday and couldn't resist getting these." She picked up the first of the boxes and handed it to Amy. Inside was a pewter-colored clutch purse with an ornate clasp.

Amy looked up at Susannah. "It's gorgeous," she said. "Thank you so much."

In the second box lay a pair of high-heeled shoes that matched her dress. Amy's eyes widened.

"I took a peek in your closet to find out what size you are," Susannah confessed.

"I don't know what to say. You've already given me so much."

Susannah gave her a hug. "It's nothing compared to what you've given us. That win today means so much to Alfredo." She straightened up and glanced at her watch. "I'd better go and get ready."

Susannah left and Amy went back to drying her hair. Once it was dry, she swept it into a loose bun and teased a couple of strands of hair so they fell in ringlets against her cheeks. Then she put on a little makeup before slipping into the dress and the amazing shoes that Susannah had given her. She stared at her reflection in the full-length mirror that hung on the wall. She slowly twirled, loving the feel of the skirt as it flared out from the tight-fitting bodice. She was ready.

She picked up her purse and took a deep breath before heading for the door.

As she rounded the curve on the staircase, she saw Alfredo standing in the front hall with his back turned to her. He was looking into the glass trophy cabinet.

"Trying to figure out where the next one will go?" Amy teased.

Alfredo turned around. His eyes widened at the sight of her.

Amy felt her cheeks turn pink as he looked over her outfit.

"You look . . . amazing," Alfredo finally managed to say.

Amy smiled shyly. "Thank you. You look pretty great yourself." Alfredo was dressed for the black-tie event in a classic tuxedo. His shoulders looked even broader than usual in the fitted jacket, and the white shirt gleamed against his olive skin.

"It occurred to me when I was getting dressed that I never asked you to be my date." Alfredo shook his head in amazement.

"Does this mean you're asking me now?" Amy asked, arching her eyebrows.

Alfredo climbed the steps to where she was standing and offered her his arm. "If you'll have me," he said softly.

Amy smiled and slipped her arm through Alfredo's. "Certainly," she answered. The two left the house, and Alfredo escorted her to the car. Soraya had been right.

Amy was ready for a summer romance, no matter how little time she had left.

🙟

The limousine had to wait in a line of cars that were dropping people off at the entrance of the country club. Pablo and Susannah sat together, enjoying a drink from the limousine's bar, and Alfredo and Amy sat opposite them.

"Chrissie's afraid you're going to put her out of a job," Pablo teased Alfredo. "She said that she had nothing to do by the time you left Impala's stall this afternoon."

Alfredo smiled. "I don't want to step on Chrissie's toes, but I'd like to start being more hands-on with all of my horses. Today showed me the difference between a horse trying for you out of obedience and a horse giving her all out of friendship."

Amy smiled at Alfredo as he reached for her hand and squeezed it.

Pablo reached forward and clapped Alfredo on the shoulder. "You have my permission to spend as much time in the stables as you want. If Impala's performance is anything to go by, you'll end up with the best string on the yard!"

Before Alfredo could reply, the door was opened by the chauffeur and the group began to pile out of the car.

Alfredo helped Amy step out onto a red carpet that covered the walkway to the country club. Laughter and music spilled out of a set of large open doors and windows as they made their way to the covered entrance with Pablo and Susannah.

Waiters and waitresses stood on either side of the carpet with trays of sparkling cider and champagne. Amy took a crystal flute of juice and walked into the entrance hall, which was lit by an enormous chandelier. Fresh flowers stood on ornate stands along the walls, and Amy breathed in their strong, sweet smell.

"So, you've finally arrived to enjoy your victory!" a stocky shaven-haired man called from the double doors on their left.

"Miguel Rodriguez, manager of the team we played today," Alfredo murmured to Amy as they followed Susannah and Pablo. Papa had chosen to stay home with Celeste and Dacil. He'd said he wasn't interested in the socializing aspect of the day, but Amy suspected that he was worn out after the emotions of the last couple of days.

"You've been lulling us all into a false sense of security with that mare of yours," Miguel said, reaching out to shake Alfredo's hand. "She's going to make a reputation for herself on the circuit this season."

Alfredo's cheekbones darkened. "Thank you, sir. But

her performance was all due to Amy's work with her."
He smiled at her.

"Is that so? Maybe I should get you to look at one or
two of my string," Miguel said, taking Amy's hand.

"Hey! Amy's allegiance is with Team Escobar, and if
she's on Long Island, she'll be staying with us!" Susannah
said with a laugh. She was looking even more stunning
than usual in a full-length cream-colored off-the-shoulder
ball gown.

"In other words, hands off!" Pablo said, grinning.

There was a small orchestra playing on a raised plat-
form at the far end of the room. Alfredo turned to Amy.
"Would you like to dance?"

Amy took his hand and let Alfredo lead her through
the crowd. Members of the country club kept coming up
to congratulate Alfredo, but he thanked them without
stopping to chat. He guided her through the ballroom
and toward the terrace.

"At last," he said as they walked out the open doors
and onto the large balcony. "I figured we'd never have
room to dance if we stayed inside!"

Lights were strung through potted trees on the deck,
and music drifted out on the warm evening air. The terrace was empty, apart from two other couples chatting
together at a table in a far corner. "You know, Susannah
was right about claiming you whenever you fly back,"

Alfredo said as they leaned against the banister. "I hope you will come visit us again." He set down his glass and turned to face her. "What you did for Impala was incredible. I'll always be in your debt."

Amy shook her head. "If you hadn't ridden Impala well today, then she would have been just as fearful as before. All I did was open the way for trust to enter your relationship."

Alfredo looked thoughtful. "Papa came to find me today as I was getting dressed for the match. He told me that every time he sees me in the saddle he's reminded of himself when he was starting his career. He said that no one else, not even my dad, makes him feel the way I do when he sees me ride. He explained it's why he has been so hard on me, because he believes I can be great." There was a note of wonder in Alfredo's voice and he smiled. "Something tells me I owe that confession to you."

Amy met his gaze and felt electricity tingle up her spine. "He was telling you the truth," she said, longing to tell Alfredo that his grandfather had one more confession to make.

Alfredo's expression grew serious. "That wasn't all Papa had to confess."

Amy's eyes widened. Papa had said that he wouldn't tell Alfredo before the match about his mother.

Alfredo stared into the night sky. "Papa decided after the match that it was time to let an extremely large skeleton out of the closet." Amy saw Alfredo's jaw clench before he continued. "Apparently, my mother *has* been trying to contact me."

"I know," Amy said, taking Alfredo's hand. "I found out a few days ago," she admitted. "But I couldn't tell you. It had to come from Papa."

Alfredo turned and placed his hands lightly on her shoulders. "You're really something, aren't you? It's like you came into my life and shined a light on all the cobwebbed corners! No wonder Papa decided to tell me."

"He didn't realize how badly you would be affected by thinking your mother had totally abandoned you," Amy said. "The moment he did, he knew he had to make things right. He's always had your best interests at heart."

Alfredo turned back to lean on the balcony. "I didn't react too well at first. I've never listed all of Papa's more unappealing qualities to his face before!" He gave a forced chuckle.

Amy could sense the hurt Alfredo was feeling. She rested her hand on his arm. "I'm sorry."

Alfredo sighed. "Susannah came to the rescue, as usual. She sat us down at the kitchen table and encouraged us to talk. I think I understand why he did what he did, but it's going to take me a while before I can forget it. But for now I'd rather concentrate on the future than the past."

"Are you going to look for your mom?" Amy asked.

Alfredo nodded. "I need to find her, if only to get closure."

Amy understood exactly where he was coming from. She hoped he found her, for both their sakes.

As the orchestra began to play a new song, Alfredo led Amy to the middle of the terrace. He slipped one arm around her waist and took her hand in his. They began moving in time to the music, and Amy felt happiness flood through her. She'd never foreseen this moment when she flew to New York.

Alfredo slowed their dance until they were just barely swaying, and Amy rested her head against his chest. She could feel his heartbeat. "By the way," he murmured, looking down at her. "I've finally chosen a name for my yacht. I want to call her *Marion*."

Amy was touched. "Thank you," she whispered.

"You're not going to rush home now that you're finished working with Impala, are you?" Alfredo asked. "I'd really like it if you could stay a while."

Amy looked up into his gaze. His eyes were intense but sparkled in the lights from the trees. "I'd love that," she admitted.

"Good." Amy thought he was going to say more, but instead he lowered his head and pressed his lips against hers.

Amy closed her eyes, caught up in the magic of the evening and Alfredo's embrace. She didn't need to say anything. She wouldn't think beyond this moment. She had taught Alfredo and Impala the importance of trust, and now it was her turn to trust in whatever the future held.

Heartland™

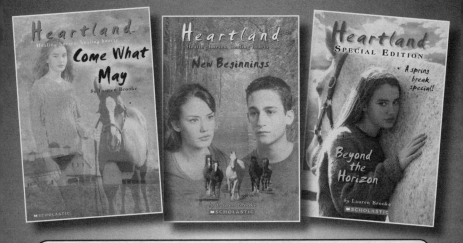

#1: Coming Home	#14: Everything Changes
#2: After the Storm	#15: Love Is a Gift
#3: Breaking Free	#16: Holding Fast
#4: Taking Chances	#17: A Season of Hope
#5: Come What May	#18: New Beginnings
#6: One Day You'll Know	#19: From This Day On
#7: Out of the Darkness	#20: Always There
#8: Thicker Than Water	Special Edition #1: A Holiday Memory
#9: Every New Day	Special Edition #2: A Winter's Gift
#10: Tomorrow's Promise	Special Edition #3: Beyond the Horizon
#11: True Enough	Special Edition #4: A Summer to Remember
#12: Sooner or Later	
#13: Darkest Hour	

scholastic.com/titles/heartland

HEARTBL

Spend some time on

Main Street

Welcome to Camden Falls   Needle and Thread   'Tis the Season

Welcome to Camden Falls   Needle and Thread   'Tis the Season

Visit www.scholastic.com/mainstreet

- ○ Explore the interactive map of Camden Falls
- ○ Hear from Flora and Ruby
- ○ Download fun scrapbooking activities
- ○ Visit Needle and Thread for craft tips

SCHOLASTIC

MSWEBSITE

More unforgettable stories from Ann M. Martin…

When their mother is taken away from them, stray pups Squirrel and Bone are forced to make it on their own—braving humans, busy highways, and all kinds of weather.

Hattie Owen didn't think her family had secrets. Until an uncle whom she never knew about showed up—and turned her world upside down.

Newbery Honor Book